THE

BREAKTHROUGH

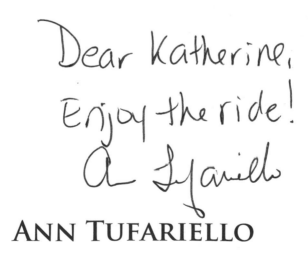

Dear Katherine,
Enjoy the ride!
An Tufariello

ANN TUFARIELLO

The Breakthrough
All Rights Reserved
Copyright © 2009 Ann Tufariello

Arctic Wolf Publishing
http://www.arcticwolfpublishing.com

ISBN-10: 0-9841233-0-X
ISBN-13: 978-0-9841233-0-8

Arctic Wolf Publishing and the "AWP" logo are trademarks belonging to Arctic Wolf Publishing
Printed in the United States of America

This book began as a bedtime story for my children. For all their love and support, I dedicate this book to my three girls and to my husband, Joe. I also dedicate the book to Mom and Dad, a daughter couldn't ask for more.

CHAPTER 1
What Did I Do?

When I opened my eyes, I was confused. I thought I was a normal kid again, tossing the football with my brother in the backyard, but I must have been dreaming. Why did I always have to wake up?

Now, as I sat cross-legged on my bed with the spindles of my headboard pressing into my back, I did what I had done each and every day for the last three weeks: I peeled flakes of paint off my headboard and flicked them into a shoebox next to my bed. Hot, salty tears stung the backs of my eyelids but I would not let them go. If I let one tear run free, I'd never stop crying. So I pinched my eyes shut and held onto them.

The sound of heavy footsteps startled me and I jumped off the bed. "Jack, come quick! I think Michael is waking up. His eyes are fluttering," my mom said, barging into my room. "I think he knows me."

This was going to be the time he finally woke up. I could feel it. All the other times were just false alarms leading up to this time.

"Michael, Michael," I cried out as I sprinted to his room. "It's me, Jack. Squeeze my hand if you know what I'm saying."

I clutched Michael's hand in mine. It felt

clammy, but human, not like the dead squid they made me dissect in biology class. Michael didn't squeeze back. His limp hand lay motionless on my trembling fingers like he was sleeping, but he wasn't.

For ten minutes, I stood at the side of the bed holding Michael's hand, imagining his fingers wiggling, but I felt nothing. Absolutely nothing.

"I swear he squeezed my hand, Jack. I know he's getting better," my mom said from the doorway.

"Ma, I'm going out."

"Look how pink his cheeks are. He looks like my little boy."

"I'm going out," I said, raising my voice.

"Where are you going?"

"To the carnival."

"Come back before it gets dark. Dad will be home soon."

"Sure, Ma," I muttered, slinking out of the room.

It was so difficult to be around my family. No one blamed me openly, but I sensed it in every bone of my body. Everyone knew I was the one who wanted to go swimming that day, not Michael. Guilt consumed me, picking away at my skin like a swarm of mosquitoes. I wanted to escape —just run away from everything.

I opened my top dresser drawer and pulled out a twenty dollar bill tucked inside a wool sock. Before the accident, I earned money mowing lawns in the summer and shoveling driveways in the winter. Not anymore. Money like everything else didn't matter.

I shoved the twenty in my back pocket. Staring in the mirror, I hardly recognized the kid gazing back at me. My face was as pale as an onion. In fact, my skin almost looked gray. My greasy brown hair hung in my eyes not having seen a comb in weeks. How could I go through the motions of each day when I didn't care about anything? I was an observer, watching the movie of my life play out in slow motion. Nothing seemed real. I wanted to stop the movie and press rewind, to change everything back to the way it was, but I couldn't.

Stepping out the front door, I nearly tripped on a heap of newspapers. I was surprised to see the sun shining after spending days inside my house with all the shades pulled down.

How could everyone go about their lives as if nothing happened? Didn't they know life would never be the same again? I didn't want to see my neighbors and their perfectly manicured lawns. My house looked abandoned with grass growing wild and shriveled up flowers lining the stone path.

I walked the two blocks to the carnival barely looking up to cross the street. As I approached the entrance, part of me wanted to turn back, but what was the use in going home? For twenty bucks, I could purchase a sheet of tickets and go on at least five rides. Five times I could forget, if only for a fleeting moment, about what I had done. So I strolled up to the ticket counter and bought the tickets.

It didn't matter what ride I jumped on. I'd go on the closest ride which happened to be the Ferris wheel—the same Ferris wheel I rode with Michael last year and the year before and the year before that. I noticed a pregnant woman waddling toward me clutching the hand of a red-haired boy.

"You aren't tall enough to ride alone. Next year you can," the woman said.

"But I want to go on it now," the boy whined, snapping his hand back.

"You can't. I'm sorry. And I can't go with you."

The boy parked his body two feet in front of me and folded his arms like Popeye. The woman glanced up, seemingly embarrassed by the kid's behavior and our eyes locked.

"He can ride with me," I offered.

"Did you hear that, Bradley? This nice boy will go on the Ferris wheel with you."

"Let's get in line," I said.

Bradley didn't say anything he just smiled at me so I assumed it was a go. When it was finally our turn, we each handed the man our tickets and Bradley elbowed me to get in first.

"Be a good boy," the woman called out.

Bradley ignored her.

"He will be," I answered, plopping into my seat. I stretched the seatbelt across our laps and tried to snap the buckle, but it didn't click the first time. I tried again. On my third attempt, I managed to lock the buckle just as the ride lurched forward. The basket lifted up a few feet and stopped again, but we still said nothing to each other. That was just fine with me because I didn't feel like talking. I could have stayed fastened in my seat all night long staring out at the park.

As our silver mesh basket circled up toward the sky, I noticed a dark, hot air balloon directly behind the Ferris wheel. I had never seen a hot air balloon at the carnival. It was probably a gimmick to sell something.

"My mom said I could take a balloon ride tomorrow," Bradley blurted out.

"I'd like to take a ride, too," I said. I wanted to scream that I'd like to float away and never come back, but I held my tongue. Bradley didn't need to hear about my problems.

As we reached the top, the Ferris wheel grinded to a halt. I was happy to stay in my seat and listen to the sounds of children screaming and laughing, but Bradley was fidgety. When we failed to move after a minute or two, Bradley began rocking the basket back and forth. I was annoyed.

"Don't jiggle the basket. We could fall out," I warned.

"No, we're strapped in. I always shake the basket."

"Bradley, please sit still."

"No. No."

Bradley slammed his back against the seat, his arms flailing. He didn't have a care in the world. The more I asked him to stop, the more he rocked. I wondered if his mother could see our basket shaking from the ground.

As I leaned toward him and struggled to hold him still, my watch caught the edge of the buckle, popping open the seat belt and sending Bradley into a fit of giggles. Then, he stood up in the basket and swayed his body like he was doing a dance. I couldn't believe it. This kid was crazy! There was no safety net. If he leaned over too far and lost his balance, he would splatter like an egg on the concrete.

"Wanna see something cool?" Bradley asked, jamming his fist into his pocket.

"Sit down. You're going to fall out. I have to fasten the seat belt."

Bradley was unfazed. He opened up his fist and revealed a small purple stone casting a grid of light across his palm. "Nothing's gonna happen with this magic rock," Bradley boasted.

I didn't know this kid. I didn't know his family. I knew nothing about him, yet I felt responsible for him. I thought of all the times my older brother had protected me. I had to protect Bradley, but I couldn't risk forcing him into a sitting position. I would reason with him.

"I'd love to see your rock after you take a seat and I fasten the belt."

"You're no fun," he teased.

"Where did you find your magic rock?" I asked, snapping the buckle as soon as he sat down.

"The guy down there with the fish. He gave it to me." Bradley pointed to the tents on the ground. As I craned my neck to get a closer look at the rock, we started moving and Bradley shoved the purple rock in his pocket. That was the last I saw of his magic rock. One more circle around and the ride was over.

"Wanna go again?" Bradley asked, hopping out of the seat.

"I have to get going," I bluffed. No way was I riding with Bradley again. So much for being nice.

I found myself wandering around the carnival alone. The sliver of joy I felt as I rode the Ferris wheel, as I marveled at the hot air balloon, was gone. Children, teenagers, even old people paced around the grounds, laughing like everything was okay. But everything was not okay. Michael should have been with me and he wasn't. The guilt and pain had returned.

"Step right up, Son. Everyone's a winner today. Just stick your hand in this fishbowl and see if you can scoop up a fish," a carnival worker cried out at me like an announcer from a TV commercial.

"I don't want to play any games today," I replied. "I'm not lucky."

"If you can scoop up a fish, you get to keep the fish and the bowl! The only catch is you're blindfolded."

"No thanks," I mumbled, avoiding eye contact.

"Oh, come on! What'd ya come here for?" the man jabbed.

I studied the carnival man. He had a nametag with the name Chuck in big red letters fastened to his blue jersey. His large tattooed arms were stretched out and he had a big, stupid grin pasted across his face. Chuck's head moved back and forth like a bobblehead. I just wanted to shut him up.

"Okay, I'll give it a try." I handed him two tickets and asked for the blindfold. He placed it over my eyes and tied it tightly.

"No peeking."

I stuck my hand in the fishbowl. The water was cold, like water from a garden hose. I swished my hand around the bowl, trying to capture a goldfish. I could feel the fish brush against my fingers, but it was a challenge to hold on to one when I couldn't see.

Suddenly, fear strangled me, squeezing the

8

breath right out of my lungs. My mind raced as I relived the nightmare from three weeks before. Thoughts swished in my mind. Waves crashed and my head whirled. I couldn't breathe. If only I could get my head up above the water, I would be able to fill my lungs with air.

I could hear my brother calling me from the shore, but my throat betrayed me. Saltwater filled my mouth drowning out my pleas for help. I waved my arms and tried to lift up my head. Over and over again, I fought to pull my head up only to have the water suck me back down. How much longer could I continue the battle? With each attempt at air, I became more convinced I wasn't going to live. My arms grew so weak, so rubbery; I could no longer feel them. A peacefulness overcame me as I surrendered to the ocean. I wasn't fighting anymore. I closed my eyes and felt warm waves pulse through me. My fears had vanished. I would die soon.

"Are you okay, Son?" Chuck asked, jolting me back to reality.

"I… I don't know what happened to me. I just blacked out," I said, trying to convince myself that nothing had happened.

"Looks like you were having some sort of nightmare or out of body experience. I saw that on TV once."

"I don't know why I got confused," I

mumbled. I didn't want to tell Chuck what happened to my brother.

"Why don't you take the fish and the bowl? Maybe your luck will change," he offered. "I wish I still had my magic rock to give you."

"Magic rock?" Where did you get it?" I asked.

"My wife found it on the floor of an ambulance. She's a paramedic. She thought it would look real pretty in a fish bowl."

"Do you think it's really magical?"

"I'd say so. When I dropped the purple rock into the bowl, the goldfish changed colors—from a grungy orange to shiny red and then a bright purple color."

"From the magic rock?"

"I didn't add nothing fancy to the water. No chemicals or nothing. Why else would the fish change colors?" Chuck asked, wrinkling his forehead.

"Where is the rock?"

"I gave it to a little boy. He was real sad 'cause he didn't get to go on the Ferris wheel."

He must have been talking about Bradley. I wished I had paid more attention to Bradley's magic rock. Maybe there was a chemical on the rock that changed the color of the fish or transformed the water. I glanced down at my goldfish gliding in the bowl. "Can I come back for my fishbowl? I can't take it on the rides."

"Sure, Son. You go have some fun now. You look like you have the weight of the world on your little back." Chuck winked at me, adding, "I'll see you around seven. Don't forget about your fish."

I walked away and almost smiled. Something about Chuck cheered me up. Staring down at the ground, I noticed a shiny red piece of paper skim the dirt. I picked it up and read the words printed at the top.

Hot Air Balloon Rides
All Labor Day Weekend
Rides Available at 7:00 am and 6:00 pm
Come enjoy the world from a new perspective!

I checked my watch. It was already 6:15 and I knew my mother would start to worry. I didn't have my cell phone—it wasn't charged anyway. If I asked to borrow a friend's phone, I would be stuck talking to the kid about Michael. It was easier just to go home. My dad had a real temper and he'd be angry if I were late. Maybe I'd come back tomorrow.

I turned toward the carnival exit, but as I did, I noticed the hot air balloon in a field to the left begging for attention. Maybe it wasn't actually begging but it sure looked awesome from a distance. I scrambled across the field to get a closer look. Although the sun was still shining, the indigo balloon appeared to be covered in glowing stars… just like the night sky. Part of me wanted to jump in the balloon basket and fly away. That would be so much easier than going home to my parents, especially my father.

Maybe I could go on the balloon. Just a quick ride. It wouldn't be dark for at least another hour. I glanced around and spotted a balloon worker crouched in the basket. His faded green baseball cap bobbed in and out of view.

"We're closed for today. Come back tomorrow morning," the man snapped. He twisted knobs and levers, barely looking up at me.

"How does this hot air balloon work? Is there some kind of engine like in an airplane?" I asked.

"No, there's no engine. It's a HOT AIR balloon! It moves because of the hot air!" the man said, standing up in the basket. He didn't exactly look like a carnival worker, more like a geeky science teacher with thick black glasses and an overgrown beard. He wasn't wearing a nametag.

"So how does the hot air make it move?"

"Look, Kid! I don't have time for the physics of hot air balloons. Why don't you just come back tomorrow? I'll answer your questions in the morning. I'm in a rush."

"I'm not trying to delay you. I want to take a ride in your balloon, but I want to make sure I don't crash. My parents don't need two kids in a coma."

"What? Who's in a coma?" the balloon man asked. He stopped what he was doing and studied my face. I was sorry I said anything but it was too late to take back my words.

"My brother almost drowned three weeks ago because of me."

Neither of us spoke for a moment. It was a sticky silence. I couldn't tell him that everything was okay because everything wasn't. The balloon man looked embarrassed but I did nothing to make him feel better. I just stared at the ground and shuffled my feet in the dirt.

"I'm so sorry about your brother," he said finally. "What was your question?'

"It's okay. I'll come back tomorrow. What time?"

"I probably have a minute to answer your question." He smiled at me.

"Thanks. I just want to know how it works."

"Do you see the gas burners under the inflated balloon?"

"Yeah."

"I press a lever to light up the burners. The hot air from the flame makes the balloon rise."

"That's it?" I asked.

"No, there's more but I really have to go."

"I thought you had rides at six in the evening. It's about 6:15 right now."

"I was heating the air in the balloon when the

winds changed. I had to close up shop for tonight. The wind has to be perfect to fly safely."

"How do you tell the balloon where to go?" I was delaying the balloon man but I kept asking questions. I couldn't help myself.

"Winds blow in different directions at different altitudes. I can maneuver the balloon sideways by moving it up or down a little and then gliding with the wind."

"And to land it?"

"If you want to bring the balloon down, you have to let some hot air escape." The balloon man winked at me. "I'll take you for a ride tomorrow and you'll see."

The man stepped out of the basket. "I have to deflate and pack this balloon. I'm supposed to meet my wife and kids at seven o'clock in town for dinner. I'm running late."

"How do you land in the same place if you can't steer the balloon too well?" I asked.

"I have a crew of balloon trackers who follow me in that pick-up truck." He pointed to a rusty, yellow truck parked in the field. I didn't notice any other balloon workers, but maybe they had left for the day.

"I'll be here first thing in the morning," I promised.

The balloon man's cell phone rang. He twitched as he pulled the phone out of his shirt pockct and answered it. Although he turned his back to me, I could hear him saying "sorry" over and over again like a little kid.

With the balloon man preoccupied, it was just me alone with the hot air balloon. I wanted to take a peek at the controls to see how it worked. Just a quick look. I stretched my neck but I couldn't make out the names on the levers. I stepped on my tippy toes and rested my chest on the basket. I still couldn't see much.

Attempting to hoist my body up onto the ledge, I fell backwards but caught myself before I wiped out. I realized in order to see the controls, I would have to get into the basket. That would be trespassing. The balloon man would never let me take a ride if I hopped into the baskct without his permission. He might even call a security guard. Or my father.

I didn't usually break rules, not that I wouldn't like to. I was always too chicken. But now I was feeling reckless. I mean, really, what did I have to lose? I already lost my brother. Why not go in the basket and have a look around?

I unlatched the lock on the basket door and stepped in. The control panel reminded me of a video game with a bunch of long words I couldn't understand. Where was the knob for lighting the flame and making it rise? It must be so much fun to blast off. I couldn't wait until the morning to take a ride.

I could see the balloon man chatting on his cell phone pacing back and forth, never looking up at me in the wicker basket. If I ducked down lower, the man couldn't see me, even if he looked over.

Attempting to crouch down in the basket, I rubbed my back against an oversized metal object. Ouch! Was I bleeding? I was so consumed with the pain in my back that I did not realize I was lifting up into the air.

CHAPTER 2
The Secret Notes

I remained crouched in the wicker basket rubbing my aching back for another moment. When the sharp pain blurred to a dull ache I lifted my head just enough to peek at the balloon man, but he was gone. Where did he go? All I could see were clumps and clumps of green bushes.

Confused, I stood up in the basket and nearly toppled over at the scene below me. I know this sounds crazy, but the balloon was floating in the air! Faster and faster the ground below dropped away from me. And I could do nothing to stop it.

The balloon man, no larger than a bug now, scurried back and forth on the concrete. I screamed for him, but he was too far away to hear my frantic cries.

Recognizing the yellow chaser truck parked near the trees, I hollered and waved my arms like a windshield wiper. Would anyone notice me? Maybe one of the balloon crewmen was still in the truck. I continued to scream, but the blaring sound of the burners drowned out my voice. I assumed bystanders thought it was just another scenic balloon lift-off. They were probably standing on the edge of the field with their cameras snapping pictures of the airborne balloon. No one knew I was a desperate kid unable to control it. The cold hard truth was: I was stuck up in the sky and had to figure out a way to bring the balloon back down without killing myself in the process.

Beads of sweat pooled on my forehead as I searched for the "Off" button. Was it the blue button, the red one or something else? What if I hit the wrong button? What if I burned the fabric and crashed to the ground? What if I smashed into a power line and electrocuted myself?

My shaking fingers pushed and pulled every button and lever on the control panel, but no matter what I did I couldn't put out the flame. The propane burners roared as the balloon climbed higher and higher into the evening sky.

I looked down at my watch but it was only 6:30. That couldn't be right—my watch must have stopped. How long would the balloon just float before it ran out of gas?

As the ground pulled away from me, tears welled up in my eyes. I wouldn't let the tears pour down my cheeks even though I might die on the balloon. Three weeks before in the ocean I had this feeling but now I didn't have my brother to rescue me.

So what do you do when you know you're going to die? When you know it's over? I'll tell you what. Listen up. After you scream and yell and shake and swallow your heart whole, you let go. You completely let go.

That's what I did.

I stopped struggling and surrendered to the thought of just floating away into nothingness. Maybe I'd fall asleep with the loud drone of the propane burners and never wake up.

I tilted my head back and looked straight up into the inflated balloon. A canopy of light cradled me like an infant. Then something clicked in me— like I flipped a switch. A warm tingling energy starting in my toes traveled through my ankles, calves, thighs, up my spine, and into my head. I couldn't tell where my body stopped and the sky began. It was crazy to think I might have died because I don't think I had ever felt so alive!

The sky, streaked with orange and reddish-purple, looked like a child colored it with crayons. I tried to figure out where my house was and the school and the park and everything else in my little town, but I could no longer recognize Mendham landmarks. All the trees, hills and streams just looked like scenery in a movie — beautiful, yet unfamiliar. And to think Michael wasn't there with me to see it.

But then, silence.

The flame from the propane burners blew out. Maybe the gas ran out or the burners broke. What did it matter? I was going down whether I liked it or not.

Down.

Down.

Down.

I could no longer see anything on the ground. I should have been frightened. I had never been in a hot air balloon let alone control one, but I felt okay— maybe even excited. Soon the sky thickened like grape jelly and everything below me was a purple blur. I kept dropping further into the squishy jelly clouds. Out of nowhere, an amusement park popped up. Just like that. No more grape jelly.

I craned my neck to get a good look at the park below me. I didn't see any people scampering on the ground. Oddly, the place looked empty but I was still too high up in the sky to know for sure. The only sound I heard was classical music, like something playing at a symphony or maybe in an elevator. No children screaming. No parents yelling at children screaming. Just beautiful music. As the carnival scene below became clearer and clearer, I became more and more confused about my location. Where was I?

I whizzed over a sparkling gold three-ringed Ferris wheel with interlocking circles in a "V" shape. The passenger baskets slid along some type of track making figure eights over and over again. Below me, I could now make out a neon yellow roller coaster shaped like a pyramid. As I soared past it, I noticed vacant cars dropping into a gaping hole in the center of the pyramid. Why hadn't I heard of this amusement park before? No one ever mentioned it. Not even Robbie Jenkins.

Robbie had been to every amusement park within a ten-state range. Why were kids keeping this place a secret? It couldn't be a traveling carnival because the rides were much too complicated to be temporary. And where were the people? I couldn't imagine an amusement park closing before seven during Labor Day weekend.

My balloon continued to float downward, almost vertically, toward what appeared to be a carousel. I couldn't see any wooden horses, but the circular shape and silver canopy suggested the ride was some type of merry-go-round. Stretching my neck to get a better look, I could now make out a single white horse on the spinning platform.

Abruptly, the hot air balloon landed smack down in the middle of the amusement park where an ice cream cart or a popcorn stand ought to be, not far from the carousel. I didn't do anything to steer the balloon. It just landed on its own with the bottom of the basket tapping the ground as if balancing on a giant sponge. I hadn't a clue where I was. Still I felt so free, so unchained, I could leap for joy.

I unlatched the door and hopped out of the basket. No hesitation. I never even looked at my watch.

Ambling toward the empty carousel, I noted how light my feet felt, as if there were springs in my shoes. The air felt flawless against my skin, neither hot nor cold.

"The other horses disappeared," a voice blurted out from the direction of the carousel. "They vanished during the Great Transition."

"What?" I wasn't sure if the speaker was talking to me but I didn't see anyone else around.

"The other horses vanished during the Great Transition," the voice said, only now I felt certain the sounds were coming from the wooden horse.

I stepped closer and studied the horse. The lips were jerking up and down like a marionette puppet and the eyes were jamming up with water as the horse whispered, "I miss them so much."

If I didn't know better, I'd think the carousel horse was alive. Ridiculous, I know. I scanned the area for a hidden camera or camera man. I saw nothing. In fact, I didn't see anyone other than the talking horse. Any moment a bunch of people would pop out from behind the balloon and start laughing at me for being so dumb. I would play along for a minute—act like I actually believed in the talking horse.

"How could the horses disappear?" I asked. "Weren't they bolted to the platform with brass poles?"

"Of course not! Why would anyone bolt an animal to a platform?" the horse shook its head back and forth. "That's downright cruel."

"But the horses are wooden," I sassed back. "They aren't alive."

22

"Everything is alive—mountains, rocks, water, carousel horses. There is awareness in everything, even on earth. Everything is energy."

"Even on earth? Where am I?" I asked, quite certain I had to be dreaming.

"This is Venus," the horse said, locking eyes with mine. "Venus jumped to the fourth dimension eons ago during the Great Transition."

"What?"

"Haven't you ever wondered about life on other planets?"

"Sure, I've seen movies."

"This isn't a science fiction movie," the horse insisted. "There is life on every planet. You just can't see it because you're in the third dimension on earth."

"But, satellite pictures show nothing."

"Because your atoms vibrate at a much slower rate than ours."

"Are you really saying I'm on Venus?"

The horse leaned toward me and slowed its speech down as if he were talking to a three-year old.

"Because we are outside of the range of human vision — like infrared lasers or ultraviolet rays — you can't see us. But we are still here. We're beyond your perception."

"We don't see extraterrestrials because they're invisible to us, is that what you're saying?"

"That's right."

"And we can't hear them?" I questioned.

"Right again. You can't touch or smell them, either."

"Wait! How can I see and hear you?" I pushed my face to within inches of the horse, my gaping mouth forming an "O" shape.

"This evening you broke through to the fourth dimension," the horse paused and stared at the empty carousel. "But if you are not careful with your thoughts, your fears will come true."

Careful with my thoughts? What was he talking about?

I examined the horse more closely, searching for a power switch. I could find nothing obvious. Still, I couldn't help but think he was a toy. He reminded me of a life-sized stuffed animal perched in a store window. Standing about four feet high on gold-tipped hooves, the horse looked immaculate. His brushed fluffy mane spilled onto a shiny white coat. His tail curled like ribbon on a birthday present. But by far, his most striking feature was his deep, indigo-blue eyes. They matched the color of the hot air balloon. I wanted to trust those eyes yet I couldn't believe what this talking horse was saying to me. Could I actually have traveled millions of miles to Venus and broken through some type of time or space warp?

"I'm sorry I didn't introduce myself before. Call me Asea," the horse said. "I'm so used to mind

24

reading I forgot you can't read mine, Jack."

Okay. That was just plain creepy. I hated the thought of anyone or anything reading my mind, even a friendly horse. Suddenly, I just wanted to be by myself. I had to admit there was a void, a loneliness, something not quite right on 'Venus'. Still, I kinda liked the abandoned amusement park because at least I could breathe fresh air—a welcome break from being cooped up in my cave of a house.

"I'm going to wander around the park," I said as I waved goodbye to Asea. I hoped my parents weren't too worried. I'd get back on the balloon before dark.

I made a beeline for the pyramid roller coaster identified by a large green sign with the words "Space Shifter" in black letters. I climbed three steps to a metal platform and observed car after car stop briefly in front of the loading zone and then take off as if there were passengers, but there weren't any. No ride attendant either. Nobody at all. Maybe it was a bad decision—but I wanted to hop on the ride. What did I have to lose?

As the next yellow car screeched to a halt, I took a deep breath. Then I climbed in and pulled the black foam body restraint over my head. It locked into place on the first try. I'd be on my way in just a moment. I could feel my heart flutter in anticipation.

What was that?

Something brushed against my leg, so softly,

so smoothly, I would have thought I imagined it, but I didn't. With my shoulders clamped down by the safety harness, I twisted my neck to see what touched me. You're not going to believe this. A three-headed snake with translucent skin was coiled around my right ankle. Three forked tongues stroked my shin. Six hooded eyes glared at me. I screamed, but no one heard me.

No one was there.

I struggled to lift the shoulder restraint but I couldn't unlock it. I pulled, pressed, jiggled then I slammed my head against the seat in frustration. The snake would bite me any minute. Any one of its three heads could do the job just fine. My blood iced up in fear.

"Are you done thrashing about like a rabid dog?" the snake hissed from one of its mouths in a hoarse female voice.

"What?" I squeaked out. I must be dreaming. Wake up! Wake up! I pinched the skin on the underside of my wrist, feeling certain I would be home safe in my bed in the blink of an eye.

I was wrong.

The snake studied me. "Are you ready to listen?" she garbled with her middle mouth as if she were sucking candy.

I swallowed hard and held my body perfectly still. I figured if the snake were talking to me she probably wouldn't bite me—at least not right away. I could buy some time.

"What do you want?" I whispered.

"I might ask you the same question."

"I want to get off of this ride."

"And—?"

"And what?"

"Is that it?" she snipped. Her eyes were flitting back and forth under her heavy eyelids, daring me.

"No, that's not it. I want to go back in time and make everything okay. I want my brother to wake up from the coma." The words tumbled out of my mouth like a runaway train.

The snake was gawking at me now. She had gotten me to admit the one thing I would die for. Now she would kill me.

"I want something too," she rasped. "I think we could be partners."

I thought surely the freakish three-headed snake was playing with me, like a cat before he rips a mouse to shreds. "How could I help you?" I asked.

The snake braided her three heads like strands of licorice and, with her long body still coiled around my ankle, propped her knot of heads on my shoe. Then she thrust out each of her tongues and said, "I know the secret."

"Secret? What secret?"

"I know how to cure your brother."

"How?" I begged. "Is it a new medicine?"

"No."

"Do you need a special machine?"

"No."

"Then what is it?" I pleaded. "How can I cure him?"

For a moment I forgot about my own danger and thought only of Michael. Could it be true? Could he be cured? I stared down at the snake, looking into each of her three sets of eyes for a sign. I felt certain she enjoyed torturing me. She was taking her sweet time answering my questions, reveling in the power she held over me. I waited, tapping my fingers on the seat.

Finally, she uttered, "The answer is locked within the secret notes."

"Where would I find them?"

"If I knew that, I wouldn't be here," the snake said. "You'll have to go back to earth to find them."

I needed to keep her mouths talking while I hatched a plan. She was in control. She knew it and I knew it.

"What do you know about the secret notes?" I asked.

"Nothing really." The snake glided her right tongue forward as if she were going to say something else, but then snapped it back into her mouth. I didn't dare move. "I might know one thing," she teased.

"What?"

"I heard a riddle eons ago. I can't recall the

28

exact words. Something like,

The notes remain inside the box
Fear controls, but truth unlocks."

"A box could be anywhere. What kind of box? A lunch box? A cardboard box? A cereal box?" I questioned.

"I can't answer that," the snake said, "but I assure you of one thing. Your brother will be cured should you locate the notes. You will activate hidden strands of DNA."

The snake was twisting her knot of heads clockwise and not glaring at me anymore. She began choking or coughing or whatever it is that snakes do. Was she preparing to bite me? I wouldn't take my eyes off of her. I had to distract her—keep her babbling.

"Got any other riddles? Anything else I should know?"

She didn't respond.

Through her see-through skin, I watched a gobstopper-sized blob climb up her middle throat. Then, with one quick shudder, her body convulsed and she spit out a purple rock. The rock, although covered in snake saliva, looked just like Bradley's on the Ferris wheel.

"This is for you," she said, placing the rock on the tongue of my sneaker.

"What's that?"

"The last Aphrodite quartz crystal. If you bring it back to earth, it will lead you to the secret notes."

"How? Is it magic?"

"The silicon in the crystal stores information." The snake paused and thrust out one of her tongues. I tensed up. "The secret notes are the key to unlocking the information in the crystal—or maybe it's the other way around." All three of her jaws opened in unison. I thought she would bite me.

She didn't.

Instead, she slurped up the crystal and began corkscrewing her disgusting sausage-like body around my right ankle. My heart beat faster and faster as I realized she must be some type of constrictor. She planned on squeezing me to death rather than poisoning me with venom. Now what?

I sucked in smaller and smaller amounts of air as my lungs broke down. I said nothing. She said nothing. I just waited, holding my breath and closing my eyes as she spiraled up toward my knee. When she reached my kneecap, I heard a clank. I opened my eyes and saw that she had dropped the spit-soaked crystal onto the seat next to my hand.

"Guard this crystal," she warned, "and find those notes."

With my eyes stuck on the snake, I watched her slither down my leg, slide under my feet, and then squirm out of sight. I never had the chance to ask the snake what was in it for her. Why exactly did she need me to find the notes? It made no sense that a snake or any other creature would give me a magic crystal without expecting something major in return. What did she need the secret notes for? And could I really cure Michael with them?

Without warning, the car heaved forward. I slipped my fingers around the wet crystal and pressed it into my jean pocket for safekeeping. I can't say I enjoyed the roller coaster ride, because I didn't. I was far too worried about the snake, the secret notes, Venus and my brother to lose myself on the ride. Actually, I couldn't wait for it to end. When the ride was finally over and the safety harness lifted on its own, I stumbled out of the car in a daze.

What was true? What wasn't? Could I have bumped my head in the roller coaster? Imagined the whole thing? Okay— if I imagined it where was I now? I should be at home in my bed if I was dreaming, but I wasn't in bed. I was standing in a strange amusement park staring at the hot air balloon in the exact place I landed.

I couldn't get back in the balloon yet because I didn't feel well. Not in a feverish way more like in a dizzy, cloudy-headed way. If the snake slithered back, I wasn't sure I would be able to outrun her.

One time when I was nine or ten I had a bad ear infection and the room was always spinning. It got to the point where I could barely make it down the stairs in the morning. That was the feeling I had now. But I was all alone.

I plunked down on a bench in front of a water fountain and waited for the cobwebs in my head to clear. The Aphrodite quartz in my pocket jabbed my thigh so I pulled it out. The crystal was shaped like a pyramid and about the size of a grape, with all four sides mirror-smooth. I liked the way the crystal felt in my fingers and the way it looked when I held it up to the sunlight. The color was a deep, translucent purple with flecks of lavender smattered throughout. I didn't get a good look at Bradley's magic rock on the Ferris wheel, but I was sure this crystal was the same type, casting the same grid of light on my palm. I could have been wrong, but I didn't think so. This just added to my confusion, but it also made me believe in the powers of the crystal, as crazy at it seemed. Of course, that meant I was on Venus and snakes and horses could talk. Still, none of that mattered. I was going to find the secret notes and cure my brother. No matter what.

But I felt uneasy.

I couldn't shrug the feeling I was being watched, observed like bacteria under a microscope. Maybe the three-headed snake returned. Or something worse.

Cringing, I glimpsed at the ground. I saw nothing but glistening blacktop. I heard nothing but the sound of my own heavy breathing. Then a crisp female voice broke the silence.

"That's my crystal," a voice said from somewhere behind me.

CHAPTER 3
The Snake Returns

I whipped my head around to see who was speaking. The words seemed to be flowing from a white marble statue in the center of the fountain, a statue of a young girl I hadn't noticed before. I couldn't determine whether the statue (girl?) was glowing or whether the sun was glowing from behind her. The weird thing was I couldn't stop staring at her—not that she was beautiful, at least not in the way movie stars are. What glued my eyes in place was her glow. I felt like a bug drawn to fluorescent light as I watched her marble lips stretch open and close.

"I hope you didn't steal that crystal," the statue warned. "A stolen crystal is worth less than a pebble of concrete."

I swallowed hard and tried to look away but her glow kept pulling my eyes back. "I didn't steal it," I whispered. "A three-headed snake gave it to me on the roller coaster."

"So a snake intercepted. A snake will tell a thousand lies. Where's the other half?" the statue snapped.

"Other half?"

"That's only half of the Aphrodite quartz. I gave the boy the whole crystal."

When she said 'boy', I thought of Bradley and

his magic rock for maybe half a second. But how could she be talking about Bradley? Crazy. "I don't know anything about the other half," I insisted, "and I haven't seen any kids here."

"No need to get paranoid. I'm not accusing you of anything." Her eyes fluttered around. "Not yet anyway." Then her face turned up in a half smile. "I'm Celeste. And you are?"

"Jack."

"Mr. Jack, what exactly are you going to do with a contaminated crystal?"

"What do you mean?"

"That Aphrodite quartz is contaminated with snake saliva and snake thoughts."

I looked down at the crystal. Maybe she was right. Or maybe she just planned to coax it out of me. "I want to bring this crystal to earth and find the secret notes."

"Secret notes?" Celeste was glaring at me like a teacher when you're caught texting in class. She shook her head a few times and mumbled something like,

**"The notes will be revealed
when the air above is healed."**

It sounded like a riddle but I couldn't ask her to repeat it. She seemed jumpy enough. In her anger, she might snatch the crystal from me.

35

"What do you know of the secret notes?" Celeste asked.

"Nothing. I just want to heal my brother."

"With my crystal?"

"M-My brother's in a c-coma," I stammered. "He was trying to save me from drowning." It was so hard to talk about Michael, even to a statue. I thought I would lose it right there. Puddles of tears pressed against the backs of my eyes but I wouldn't let them out. I swallowed hard and blinked a few times. The statue was still staring at me but now it looked like she was the one about to cry. At first, I thought mist from the fountain moistened her eyes, but soon I knew better.

Water gushed from her stone eyeballs, streamed down her cheeks, and dripped onto her feet. The next thing I knew, the statue was morphing into a living girl. Just like that. Waves of platinum blonde hair skimmed her shoulders, falling loosely on her sundress. Her chiseled face softened, her stone exterior became translucent skin. Was Celeste going to pounce on me? I squeezed the crystal a little tighter. I noticed her glow was gone.

"You don't trust me," she said, sniffling.

"I-I-I do. It's just—" I paused, feeling heat flush my cheeks. Her tears seemed genuine but I wasn't taking any chances. I shoved the Aphrodite quartz back into my pocket.

"Now you've done it, Mr. Jack. Why did you

have to tell me the sad story about your brother?" She paused to wipe tears beading along her chin. "You stirred up feelings in me. I wanted to remain frozen. Blissfully numb."

I had no idea what Celeste was talking about, but getting defensive wasn't going to help. I knew that much. "I didn't mean to upset you," I said. "You can go back to being a statue. I'll leave."

"Don't you want to know why I'm crying?"

"Only if you want to tell me."

"My family disappeared. They were using crystals and searching for the secret notes when they vanished. My older brother, Prion, believed the secret notes were hidden on earth." She paused, closing her eyes. "He yearned to grow wings and fly to earth."

"Why earth?"

"Thousands of years ago ancient Venusians traveled to earth and learned secrets," she said, tilting her head back and gazing up at the sun. "In the days before the Great Transition, my siblings were using large, powerful crystals to harness pure energy. Things kept getting worse and worse."

She hopped down from the fountain and sat down next to me, her chalky skin the color of toothpaste. Celeste began speaking with short, halted breaths. "Before, we had so many fears. Fear there wasn't enough. Fear of disease. Fear someone would kill you before you could kill them."

As her voice grew louder and more deliberate,

I could feel my chest tighten. Celeste was speaking faster now making my ears buzz. "All of these fears caused intense greed, hatred, and war. We burned gobs of fossil fuel creating a layer of trapped gas."

I drew in a breath but the air tasted poisonous—like I was part of Celeste's story. My stinging eyeballs clouded up so I closed them. She babbled on, "The oceans boiled, thickening the sky with more toxic vapor. Soon, carbon dioxide from liquefied rocks escaped into the atmosphere."

Then, she fell silent. I crossed my right leg over my left, uncrossed them, and then crossed them again. I opened my eyes and saw Celeste bawling, her face thick with tears.

"In a blink, Venus jumped to the fourth dimension, but my family was gone. They abandoned me."

"Maybe they didn't *choose* to leave you," I blurted. "Maybe they're trapped."

"Stuck on earth?" she asked, scrunching her face. "Unable to cross into this dimension?"

I nodded.

Celeste lifted her eyes deep in thought. After a moment, she asked, "You want the secret notes, right?"

I nodded.

"I have an idea."

"You do?"

"Maybe we could help each other, Mr. Jack."

"How?"

"You could purify the tainted crystal and carry it back to earth on the hot air balloon."

"How would that help you?" I asked.

"My siblings would be drawn to the silicon in the crystal like steel to a magnet. They could help you find the secret notes. They must have some idea where they're hidden."

"But if they're trapped on earth, I'm not sure I can help them."

"It's not what *you* can do; it's what the *crystal* can do." Celeste's human body beamed with light like nothing I've seen before. (Okay, maybe in a movie.) Either she was truly happy or she was setting me up.

"Purify the crystal in the four basic elements: water, fire, air, and earth. The crystal's powers will astound you."

"How do I do that?" I asked, pressing my palms on my legs to stop them from jiggling.

Celeste stared into space. I could almost see her thoughts rise like steam off summer pavement. She waited a moment before speaking. "The element earth is obvious. Bury the crystal in the earth when you return home. But fire and air have me stumped."

"And water?" I asked.

"Simple. Dip the Aphrodite quartz in the fountain."

That sounded easy enough. Maybe a little too

easy. Was it possible Celeste was tricking me? If I dunked the crystal in the water, she'd wrestle it away from me. Finders keepers, losers weepers. I'd be left with nothing and no chance of saving my brother. Maybe if she could get her hands on the crystal she'd go to earth herself. Then again, purifying the crystal made sense. The Aphrodite quartz probably was contaminated with snake gook.

I reached into my pocket and plucked out my precious crystal. With it pinched tightly between my thumb and index finger, I swished my hand back and forth in the fountain. The water felt cool but not cold. Then I did something stupid. I leaned over too far. Before I could catch myself, I fell into the fountain and dropped the Aphrodite quartz. If the water were clear like in a swimming pool, I could have grabbed the crystal. But no. The moment the crystal touched the water, the water turned to grape juice. I couldn't see the crystal. A wave of panic washed through me. I needed that crystal if I was ever going to uncover the secret notes. *Breathe*, I told myself.

I would just have to fish around for the crystal. It had to be there somewhere. The purple water was only two feet deep. I circled the fountain on my hands and knees over and over, but I couldn't find it. My chest muscles tightened as I became more desperate. Then something sharp poked my kneecap. As I lifted my knee to grab what I thought would definitely be the crystal, I noticed a crack in the fountain floor next to the pedestal base. I pressed my face against the crack and tried to peer through the hole. I couldn't see much but I knew the crystal slipped through the crack because I saw a grid of flickering light in some kind of tunnel. Was the crystal leading me to the secret notes?

I lifted my head out of the water and tried to make eye contact with Celeste, but she cast her eyes down in shame like a kid caught lying. She was hiding something—that much I knew—but I needed the crystal. Nothing, absolutely nothing, would stop me from getting it and finding the secret notes.

"I didn't want to tell you about the labyrinth," she confessed. "Earth beings are not ready for it."

"A labyrinth like a maze?"

"A maze is not a labyrinth. With a labyrinth, there is only one way in and one way out. No dead ends," she explained. "But you can't go down there. It's too much for earth minds."

"I have to find the crystal," I insisted.

"Don't you think I want you to get that crystal? I want you to go to earth and find my family, but I can't let you go down there. I can't live with that kind of guilt."

"Please," I begged.

"The last earth being to touch that Aphrodite quartz never completed the task. Something spooked him down there." Celeste shook her head back and forth. "I never saw the boy again."

"If I find the crystal, I promise I will look for your family. Please, please tell me how to get down there." I reached to touch her arm expecting to feel skin, but her arm felt solid like a cast. "Don't morph back without telling me."

It was too late. I watched the soft lines of her dress harden like cement against her marble legs. Her face, soft and giving only seconds before, turned to stone with her eyes turned down. Would she say something? Oh, please, say something.

"I'll search for your family if you tell me," I bargained.

Her mouth gurgled. "Under the—"

"Under what?"

"Carousel," she panted. With that last word her lips stuck together in a frown. I sprinted toward the carousel never looking back at Celeste. I hoped the horse would still be there. Maybe he'd go into the labyrinth with me.

"Asea," I called out in desperation. He didn't respond. I didn't have time to look for him. I'd have to go alone.

Not quite sure what I was looking for, I hopped up on the spinning platform and toddled toward the center. The trap door had to be there somewhere but where? After three or four complete turns, my stomach felt so queasy from looking down I nearly tripped on a black, metal knob jutting up from the wood. The trap door! I dropped to my knees and gave the knob a yank, wrenching the door open on the first try.

Streams of purple light blinded me. Although I could see nothing, I knew my crystal was still there! And that alone kept me going as I made my way down at least twenty narrow steps. Once I reached the bottom of the staircase, I could see that the crystal lay only feet away from me—or so I thought. I could almost feel the smooth stone in my fingers. The crystal seemed to be the only light in the labyrinth, but its glow was so intense, it might as well have been daylight underground.

But then something strange happened. As I crouched down to scoop the crystal, my face smacked into a wall, a transparent glass wall. I flinched in pain. When I was five or six years old, I bolted through a sliding glass door chasing Michael and ended up in the emergency room with thirty-seven stitches. At least this time I only bruised my cheek.

Just thinking about having fun with Michael made my eyeballs burn, but this was no time to start crying. I had to remain focused and figure out how to get the crystal on the other side of the glass wall. There had to be a path. Yes, of course. Celeste said this was a labyrinth. I only needed to find the opening. Easy enough.

With my hands stretched out in front of my face like a mime's, I pressed the glass surrounding me until I discovered an opening on my right. Then I gradually twisted along the path, never quite sure if I was getting any closer to the crystal. Finally, when I wasn't more than a foot away from the crystal, I stretched my arm out and lunged at the glistening Aphrodite quartz.

It wasn't there.

My fingers passed through empty space.

I lunged again.

Nothing. I could feel my heart churning in my chest as I realized the crystal was an optical illusion. Where was the real Aphrodite quartz?

"I told you to hold onto the crystal, but you didn't listen," a familiar voice hissed. I could feel cold air swirl around my ankles—probably a triple dose of snake breath.

I had nowhere to go. No clue how to escape the glass labyrinth and I didn't want to leave without the crystal. I tried to swallow back the bitter taste in my mouth, but it stuck to my tongue. Now what? Without dropping my head, I glanced at the snake only inches away from my feet and sucked in as much air as I could hold onto.

"I ought to rid myself of you right here right now," she rasped with her left mouth. "Why didn't you return to earth as I instructed?"

"I-I-I wasn't feeling up to the balloon ride," I stammered. "But I'm going back to earth now."

"It's too late. You've entered the forbidden glass labyrinth. You're hooked."

"I can turn around and climb out and jump on the balloon," I said trying to convince myself as much as her.

"No. You cannot," she snapped. "You must retrieve the Aphrodite quartz before you can return home. How will you cure your brother if you cannot even help yourself?" Her six hooded eyes narrowed. "Why did I trust you to find the secret notes?"

"But I don't know where the crystal is."

"I know where it is," she taunted. "I don't know if I should tell you. Perhaps another earth being is better suited to the task."

"Please tell me where the crystal is," I begged.

"Very well. I will give you another chance just this one time." She slowed her speech down savoring each word as it floated out of all three mouths in unison. "The Aphrodite quartz is in the Galactic Library at the center of this labyrinth."

"I saw the crystal here only a moment ago," I said, pointing to the empty space.

"Foolish child, your crystal is in the holographic wing of the library. Reclaim it before someone else does."

She slithered around my feet making a figure eight with her body as her heads spun around and around. And then she disappeared.

Completely.

Poof.

Could the three-headed snake be a hologram too? She never actually touched me in the labyrinth but I could have sworn I felt her cold breath blow against my ankles. If she was a hologram that would mean she was in the holographic room of the library with my Aphrodite quartz. I would have to face her again if I ever wanted to see my crystal.

But let's be honest—did I have a choice? No. Even if it meant tangling with the snake, I was determined to get the crystal back, find the notes, and cure Michael.

With that determination, I gradually made my way through the glass labyrinth. You never knew when that creepy snake would pop out with her three icky heads.

CHAPTER 4
Get Me Out of Here

As the Galactic Library came into full view, I was struck by the sheer size of the building. When I first entered the glass labyrinth, the library appeared to be a piece of glittering candy off in the distance. Now, only feet away from the front steps, I felt like a small child before a grand palace. I could make out at least four spiraling towers in vibrant red, orange, yellow and green. Two large rounded pillars on either side of the white marble front doors created a majestic entrance fit for a royal family. I lifted my gaze and observed rows of diamond and octagonal shaped windows lined up like a checkerboard above the front entrance. Chinks of light beamed through the windows creating geometric patterns on the ground around my feet. The front doors, a glistening white like fresh snow, stood at least twelve feet high.

I climbed the steps two at a time, stopped on the landing, cupped my ear, and pressed it against the crack between the doors. I don't know what I expected to hear: keyboards clicking? feet shuffling? the three-headed snake? I heard nothing. Maybe that was good. I could get the crystal back before anyone noticed.

Drawing in a deep breath, I tugged on the iron handle of the door to the right. The door was much lighter than I would have guessed, like it was made of cardboard. I stepped into the foyer area and had a look around. The room continued on and on in every direction. In fact, I couldn't see any walls. Rows and rows of books in gigantic iron bookcases stretched toward the ceiling like skyscrapers. People (Venusians?) were scattered throughout the spacious room but no one took notice of me. These were the first normal looking people I had seen since I landed on Venus.

I stepped across the black and white checkered floor with only the squeaks from my sneakers breaking the stillness. I figured there would be a map or at least a few signs like in a real library or museum. I could find nothing, just endless rows of bookcases. I circled around and around searching for the holographic room but everything looked the same. Finally, I tapped an old man on the shoulder.

"Do you know where the holographic room is?" I asked in my polite kid voice.

He kept his head buried in a book never looking up at me. I thought that was pretty rude but maybe he was deaf.

Next, I approached a young girl, not much older than me, with black hair half way down her back pulled in a loose ponytail. Like the old man, she leaned against a bookcase, her face pressed into the pages of a brown leather book.

"Excuse me, Miss. Where would I find the

holographic room?"

She didn't respond. Maybe she spoke another language. Could she be deaf too? After two or three more people completely ignored me, I began to think I was invisible. I wasn't asking for money just directions. Then, the clicking sound of slippers smacking against the marble caused my shoulder muscles to tense up.

"May I be of assistance? You look confused," a man said, popping out from behind a bookcase. "Call me Fagan. I'm head librarian."

Fagan was older than my parents, maybe fifty or sixty years old on Earth. A clump of gray-streaked hair rested on top of his pointy head. He wore dusty overalls with a maroon plaid flannel shirt peeking out from behind the straps—not your typical librarian clothes. Fagan looked vaguely familiar, like a distant relative in an old photo. Maybe I dreamed of him. I closed my eyes, struggling to remember his face. Who was he? I was sure I would place his face once I stopped trying so hard. As he turned, I caught a glimpse of his profile and knew instantly who he looked like—the balloon man! Fagan appeared to be an older likeness of the balloon man, like a computer-aged photo, but his eyes were the same deep brown. Somehow I felt safer and more relaxed, as if Fagan and I were close friends.

"I thought no one could see me," I said, shifting my weight back and forth between my feet.

"The others are too busy studying their books," Fagan replied. "They're in another world, so to speak."

"I'd like to go to the holographic room."

"You do? What an interesting request from an earth being."

"How do you know I'm from earth?"

"Your energy gives you away."

"Do you see many people from earth?" I asked.

"No. On occasion, an earth being will break through the heaviness of the third dimension in a dream and end up here." Fagan studied my face and I twitched in embarrassment. "Have you been here before? You feel so familiar?"

"No."

"How do you know about the holographic room if you've never visited the library?" he asked, wrinkling his forehead.

"I lost something in the fountain that tumbled down here—or at least I hope it landed here."

"What did you lose?"

I didn't want to tell him. I really didn't. I wasn't that stupid. But if I didn't tell him about the crystal, he might not show me to the room. Then I'd never get the Aphrodite quartz. If I did tell him, he might snatch it from me, but then again he might not. Somehow I felt comfortable with Fagan

"I dropped a crystal," I whispered.

"What kind?"

"A lavender Aphrodite quartz."

"That's who you look like." Fagan drew his hand to his face and tossed his head back. "The boy with the Aphrodite quartz. You're the spitting image of him—maybe a little younger. You have the same voice, the same movements."

I could feel the blood drain from my head, as if I stood up after doing a headstand. Everything was crashing around me. If I didn't know better, I'd think he was talking about Michael. But how could he know Michael? I thought of Bradley's crystal on earth. Could Michael have visited Venus before me and gotten the crystal? The whole story seemed so far-fetched. Michael would have said something to me.

"Are you okay?" Fagan asked. "You can take a seat, if you need to." He gestured toward a black lacquer chair a few feet away.

"I'm fine. Can you take me to the holographic room?" I wasn't ready to talk about Michael yet. I needed that crystal.

"Follow me."

We passed bookcase after bookcase, each extending up at least twenty feet. As we strolled by the bookcases I tried to read the titles on the spines, but I didn't think they were written in English. My eyes lingered on a dark burgundy leather-bound book with dusty gold letters that teetered on the edge of the shelf.

"That's not you," Fagan said, shaking his head.

"What?"

"Those books concern the lives of other beings, not your life."

"What's in my book?" I asked.

"Everything you have ever seen or experienced. Future possibilities too."

"The book is like a crystal ball?"

"No. There are many possible futures. You can explore different scenarios and make choices accordingly. I must warn you, though. Earth beings tend to get addicted to this library."

"What do you mean?" I questioned.

"You will struggle to make decisions once you taste the knowledge of the Galactic Library."

He had to be exaggerating. At least that's what I told myself as I strolled down the aisles, passing row after row of books. I grew more curious about the names. Who were these people? Did they live on earth in ancient times? Or were they still alive? Maybe they lived on other planets or in other galaxies.

Without warning, an oversized maple brown leather book dropped onto my right toe, shooting jolts of pain through my foot. I ripped my shoe off and clutched my throbbing toe while hopping on my left foot. After a moment I put my sneaker back on and tied my ratty shoelaces, but something caught my eye while I stared down at the gleaming floor. The title of the book was Michael Anthony Barton- born on December 14th, in Morristown, New Jersey!

I lunged for the book. Fagan stopped me before I could open it. He flashed a disappointed look. "You can't read other people's books."

"What? I just wanna—"

"No, it cannot be done." Fagan shook his head. "Come along."

"Okay," I grumbled following him.

If I could only get my hands on that book, I'd know how Michael felt, whether he would get better and whether he'd ever walk again. I'd know everything. I had to take a look. I just had to. Twisting my shoulders, I glanced back toward the spot where I saw his book. The next thing I knew a mound of books tumbled off the shelves and buried Michael's. Could I run back and find it? Fagan had walked several steps ahead and was not within sight, but I could hear his clicking slippers. I chickened out.

"Here you are," Fagan said pointing to a small dark room.

I peered into the room. Beams of light scattered across the floor in every color of the rainbow. There were colors I had never seen before. I kept blinking trying to focus on the objects in the room, but everything was so blurry. It was as if I had picked up another kid's glasses and put them on. All I could make out were the grids of intense color.

"How will I find the crystal? I can't see much," I said, standing at the edge of the room.

"You can see me."

"Everything else is fuzzy."

"Things will come into focus as your eyes adjust. Be patient." Fagan turned to leave.

"Wait. Don't go. Do you know anything about the secret notes?" I panted, touching his shoulder. "Once I get the Aphrodite quartz back I have to find the secret notes."

Fagan's face turned ashen white, his cheeks tightened and the veins in his neck popped out. "I do," he mumbled, jerking his head back and forth, "but I'm afraid to say."

"You have to tell me. I need to cure my brother."

"You have a brother?" Fagan asked, studying my face again.

"He's in a coma at home."

"He is? Are you certain?"

"My brother nearly drowned saving me. I'm certain."

"Time is more compressed here, like a dream. He might not be where you think he is."

My mind sputtered. Was Fagan trying to change the subject so he wouldn't have to tell me anything about the secret notes? Maybe. Still, I was beginning to think that Michael had visited Venus and had traveled to the Galactic Library. I tried to sort out a possible scenario in my head. This was the best I could do:

1.) Michael visited Venus somehow.

2.) He met Celeste at the fountain and she gave him an Aphrodite quartz crystal.

3.) He dropped or lost half of it before he left Venus.

4.) Michael returned to earth with only half the crystal.

5.) The carnival man at the fish booth got Michael's crystal from his wife in an ambulance—I think that's what he said.

6.) The carnival man gave the crystal to Bradley.

"I really have to go," Fagan said, jolting me out of my daydream.

"But the crystal—how will I find it in this room?"

"If it's here, you'll find it."

"And the secret notes? How will I find them?"

Fagan's face contorted again. "Any being searching for the secret notes has perished. Are you certain you want to find them?"

"I don't care about my own safety—only about my brother."

"You must help yourself before you can help him." Fagan turned his back to me.

I watched Fagan disappear behind a row of bookcases although I could still hear his slippers smacking against the floor. When the sound faded to a dull click, I turned back toward the holographic room. I had to get that crystal even if I couldn't see anything. I had no choice. Taking one step into the room, I remembered the snake and pulled my foot back before my toe tapped the floor.

"Where are you going?" the snake grunted.

My vision was so poor, so distorted; she appeared to have nine heads rather than three. I wiggled my eyeballs in their sockets trying to focus on the snake.

"I wasn't always this hideous, you know. You don't have to mock me with that smirk," she said.

"I'm not laughing at you. I can't see well."

"I repulse you."

"You don't."

"I could devour you whole," she threatened with her left mouth.

"I know," I mumbled.

"But I won't. At least not now. I need you to find those secret notes."

I breathed a sigh of relief and my vision began to clear. I could now see the crystal balancing on the snake's middle tongue. I knelt down on the floor with my right palm face up and braced myself for whatever the snake would do next. She didn't bite me, or even touch my skin. She simply spit the

Aphrodite quartz into my hand like a cherry pit. I wrapped my trembling fingers around the crystal, ignoring the snake saliva. It felt smooth and warm to the touch. I jammed the crystal deep into my front jean pocket. I needed to get away from the snake before she changed her mind.

"Do you think the notes could be in this library?" I asked on a whim.

She twisted her whole body toward me. "Why don't you take a peek at your book?" the snake teased. "There may be some clues about the secret notes in your book."

"My book?"

"It's probably shelved near your brother's."

She seemed to know everything except the location of the secret notes. What did she need me for? Was I a fool to trust her? Would she dispose of me as soon as she got the secret notes? I crammed those thoughts down.

"How do you know where my brother's book is?"

"Never mind the details. Go find your book and see what you can learn. You're quite fortunate to have the option to examine your book."

"Fortunate?"

"I never had the opportunity and now look at me. I'm revolting."

I tried not to stare at her. I didn't want to upset her any further. I sensed she wanted me to reassure her but I couldn't. The snake babbled on. "I made a dreadful decision a long time ago and now I continue to pay for it."

"What kind of decision? I've made some horrible choices myself."

"Let's not get all chummy here. Stick to the task at hand. "

"Is that why you're searching for the notes? Are you trying to change your past?"

"That's none of your business," she hissed.

Realizing I had touched a snake nerve, I changed the subject. "Maybe I should take a quick peek at my book."

"Excellent choice. Now I must go before I am seen in this hideous condition," the snake remarked. She slithered away with all three heads curved down like the hook of a coat hanger.

I turned to search for my book. Every bookcase was as neat and orderly as the next. Would the books be shelved alphabetically? By age? By location? There had to be millions of books in the Galactic Library, maybe billions. I crouched down near a bookcase and examined the titles looking for some kind of filing system.

"What did I tell you about inspecting other people's books? You cannot look at anything but your own," Fagan snipped. He must have been watching me.

"I know. I'm searching for my own book," I

insisted.

"I am the librarian. I hand out the books. This is not a do-it-yourself hardware store. This is the Galactic Library."

"I'm sorry."

"State your full name," Fagan commanded like a robot.

"John Joseph Barton."

"Jack is a nickname?"

"Yes."

"What is your birthday?"

"January 12th."

"Capricorn, eh?"

"Yes."

"And your place of birth?"

"Morristown, New Jersey," I answered, surprised by how shaky my voice sounded out loud.

"That's right here," Fagan said.

He reached up onto his tippy toes and handed me a large brown leather book with my name typed in boldface letters on the cover. My hands trembled as I clasped the book with my fingers. Did I really want to know everything about my life?

"Have a seat," Fagan said pulling up a wooden chair from behind the bookcases. I sat down and inhaled deeply, trying to still my nerves, but my bent fingers shook uncontrollably.

"How will I know the right page?" I pressed the book against my chest.

"When a surge of warm energy travels through your body, open the book to any page. Don't be afraid. Fear jumbles everything."

I pinched my eyes shut and tried to do as he instructed. My mind kept drifting back to my brother and all of the trouble I caused him. Why did I have to go swimming that day? I tried to think happy thoughts. Honestly I did. I tried to remember all of the fun Michael and I had.

When my hands stopped shaking and I felt reasonably calm, I rested the book on the tips of my fingers. I could feel something warm bubbling from my toes up my calves. That must be the sensation Fagan was talking about. I popped the book open and peered into a random page, the image fuzzy at first. But a strange thing happened, something that scared me. I began to feel tension rotate through me, twisting from my left side to my right and back around to my left. I should have slammed the book shut, but something made me look. Why? I'll never know.

Saltwater flowed up my nostrils, blocking my air supply. My arms were so floppy I didn't have the strength to raise them out of the water. I stopped fighting it. I could feel my body getting lighter and lighter. Without warning, a hand grabbed me from under my arms, jolting me out of the peacefulness. I thought I had drowned and now an angel escorted me to a heavenly paradise. The angel's fingers pressed into the flesh covering my ribs, but it didn't hurt much.

Now I could see that my rescuer was Michael and not an angel. His facial muscles twisted in pain as he battled the waves while still clutching me under his right arm. The shoreline appeared so close, but we weren't making any progress. A lifeguard, at first only a pinpoint in the distance, moved toward us in a small canoe. As she approached us, she tossed out a round flotation device, but we couldn't latch onto it. Another lifeguard joined the rescue attempt with a second boat a few feet behind. The female lifeguard positioned her canoe within inches of us and struggled to pull me into her boat. As the other rescuer attempted to hoist Michael into his canoe, a gigantic wave crashed onto us. My brother slipped under. A moment later, the lifeguard dragged Michael's limp body onto the canoe.

"No. No. No," I hollered.

Immediately I found myself in the Galactic Library with my book in my hands. Snapping the book closed, I thought back to that day three weeks before. Michael was always there for me. And look what I had done.

"I have to leave," I said, handing the book to Fagan.

"But there's more. You can see waves of possibilities in the future if you study your life's book," Fagan recited like an infomercial. "You can learn from future mistakes."

"And past ones," I whispered, "but I don't want to know."

"Aren't you just a little curious?" Fagan asked. "You said you wanted clues about the secret notes."

I shoved my fingers into my jean pocket and stroked the crystal with the tip of my pinky finger. I tried to convince myself that if I could hold a strong mental image of the secret notes, I'd flip to the right page. Using my left index finger, I retraced the name on the book, still too frightened to crack it open again. What if I learned something terrible about myself? Horrible, dark thoughts plagued me. The more I tried to squash them, the more fiercely they fought to survive. Over and over I repeated to myself, *where are the secret notes*? *Where are the secret notes?* I repeated the words so many times that the individual syllables no longer made sense.

"I'll take another peek."

"Please," Fagan said, offering the book.

I clasped it in both hands and drew in a deep breath. Then I opened my book somewhere in the middle. I lifted my eyelids, the image of Michael playing football with his friends in our backyard came into focus.

A soft rain kissed the ground but no one

seemed to notice. It had to be mid-autumn because the leaves were changing colors and the grass had that yellow burned look. Michael looked the same age—about fifteen. I didn't recognize the maroon striped rugby shirt he was wearing but I knew his Mets baseball cap. I had borrowed it more times than I could count.

"Jack, tell them to come in. It's going to pour any minute," my mom said from somewhere inside the house.

I tried to pull the words up my throat to answer my mother, but I couldn't. My throat, my arms, my legs, everything was frozen. Floating in some type of dream state, I could feel my inner being pull out of the picture. I was only an observer now.

Tommy Sage was covered in mud waving his arms frantically for the ball, but I don't think Michael could see that he was open. My brother threw the ball to another teammate, someone I couldn't make out. The ball skimmed across the kid's fingertips and skidded onto the wet ground, rolling into Mr. Jenkins' cornfield behind our house. Mr. Jenkins would be furious if he saw teenagers traipsing through his property for a ball or anything else.

As I watched another kid scramble to retrieve the ball, I noticed a purple grid of light beaming from the field. The crystal! Someone had buried or dropped an Aphrodite quartz in the space between

63

my backyard and Mr. Jenkins' cornfield. The purple glow was unmistakable.

Then I did something really stupid. I reached into my pocket and stroked the crystal. Abruptly, I found myself back in the Galactic Library clasping my book, as if a giant vacuum sucked me out of the future and dumped me in the library. I wanted to dive into that page with Michael playing football and never close the book. Never go back to earth. Just stay there. Forever.

I needed to get back to that page and find out where the crystal was buried. Clutching the book in my hands, I noted the smooth leather touching my fingertips. I closed my eyes and thought of my parents. My father would be ecstatic to have his older son back and my mother would never need another thing as long as she lived. I would never fight with my brother again. We would be so happy. I froze that perfect thought in my mind. When a negative image popped up, I crammed it down.

Cracking the book open, I flipped through the pages until one felt warm to the touch. I couldn't wait to see a future scene with Michael healthy. At first the image was out of focus, but then my eyes adjusted.

This was not what I wanted to see.

My mother stood in the hallway upstairs in ripped jeans and a black bulky sweatshirt I didn't recognize. Her face, red and swollen from crying, looked older almost like my grandmother's, yet I knew she wasn't too old—she just looked it from the gallons of tears. Her hair, frizzy and streaked with gray, did not suit her. The most striking difference, however, was her bony frame. She appeared as if she hadn't eaten in weeks, like a whiff of wind would blow her over.

"He's gone. He's gone," she kept saying, stroking her face with her fingers.

I wanted to say something to comfort her, but the words died on my lips. I could hear my father shouting from downstairs at no one in particular—at the world in general. With my chest muscles clamping down, air was hard to come by.

I pinched my eyes shut and slammed the book in my lap. I didn't need to see anymore—I had seen enough of life without Michael. I had to get home before that future scene became the present.

"What did you see?" Fagan asked.

"Where's the exit?"

"You can't leave yet. What about the secret notes? Isn't that why you opened your book?"

"Get me out of here," I said, scanning the room for the front door.

"Wait. I might know something about the secret notes," Fagan confessed. "Something about light."

"What about light?"

"I'm trying to remember."

"I thought you didn't want me to search for them," I said.

"It's your free choice not mine. I'm just a librarian."

"I really have to go."

"I'm sure we'll meet again," he called out.

I never looked back at Fagan.

CHAPTER 5
The Journey Back

I had no idea where I was going, but I had to get out of there. I sprinted through the library trying to retrace my steps, but clearly I was running in circles. Every iron bookcase looked the same. There were no exit signs or maps or information booths— only Venusians with their faces buried in their books. I should have asked Fagan to escort me to the exit. Now I didn't even know where he was.

After several misguided attempts, I stumbled upon the front door. I bolted down the front steps two at a time as if a psycho were chasing me. When I reached the bottom step, I found myself standing in the glass labyrinth but I couldn't just run through the glass. I had forgotten that small detail. What now? After a moment of panic, I remembered the Aphrodite quartz.

I yanked the crystal out of my pocket and held it at eye level. It felt warm to the touch, even warmer than usual. On the glass walls surrounding me, I noticed beams of purple light spliced in spider web patterns.

Using the light beams as my guide, I was able to make my way through the labyrinth. I could pass through any space where I didn't see a spider web design. It was as simple as that. Soon, I reached the steps leading me up to the carousel. I was almost there! As I climbed the steps I thought of nothing but the hot air balloon. It should be next to the carousel. It had to be there.

I flung open the trap door and popped my head out. There it was—in the exact same spot where I had last seen it. The splendid hot air balloon.

I unlatched the lock on the basket and climbed in, but I had forgotten another small detail. How was I going to get the balloon moving? I hadn't thought of that when I raced out of the Galactic Library. Maybe I'd get lucky.

Squatting in the basket, I flipped the control panel switches—up, down, right, left. Nothing happened. I did it again. Still no change in the balloon. *Think positive*, I reminded myself. I closed my eyes and imagined being home with my parents and brother. Everyone was smiling and laughing in my dream. I drew in a deep breath and slowly exhaled.

With a soft swish, the balloon lifted off the ground. No loud propane burners. No burning flame. Just a peaceful upward movement like a giant helium balloon soaring into the sky. The balloon had lifted up eight or ten feet when I reached into my right pocket for the crystal.

It wasn't there.

I checked my left pocket. Not there either. My hands trembled as I turned my jean pockets inside out, but where was the crystal? When did I have it last? I knew I had it in the glass labyrinth. But then what? I couldn't remember what I did with the Aphrodite quartz as I climbed the steps to the carousel. How could I be so careless, so nonchalant as if I had a hundred crystals waiting at home for me? Could I have dropped it? I didn't hear any clinks when I jumped off the wooden platform. One thing was certain: there was no point in returning to earth without the crystal. I had to go back and find it.

Drifting upward slowly, my balloon hovered over a sunflower field adjacent to the carousel. Fields of flowers stretched in every direction, in colors I had never seen on earth. But rather than be dazzled by the beauty, I was sickened by the smell. All I could think of was a funeral parlor which made me think of a coffin. I didn't want to think beyond that. I knew what I needed to do. I needed to shut the burners off and coax the balloon down. But after a few lame attempts, I realized I couldn't stop the soaring balloon. I would have to jump if I ever wanted to see the crystal again.

I looked down and studied the ground. It was a big drop. More than ten feet. I could feel a burst of adrenaline surge through my body. Since I had a lot of experience jumping off the roof of my backyard shed, I knew I could do it. I needed that crystal.

Far more confident than I had any right to be, I climbed out of the basket and perched myself on top of the basket rim. Still clutching the inside of the rim,

I dangled my body along the side of the basket for a moment. The cane strips picked at my bare stomach and the weight of my body put aching pressure on my wrists. This left me with two choices: climb back in the basket or jump. It was now or never. Simple as that. After counting to three, I pinched my eyes shut and let go.

As I plunked down onto the field, every bone ached, every muscle throbbed. I wanted to scream, to wail, to cry and cry, but I would not give up yet. Not here. Not now. Instead I stretched out on my back like a dying cockroach and gazed up at the nearly perfect lavender sky. I couldn't go home now even if I wanted to. My hot air balloon had drifted away.

Laying in the field, I half-expected the three-headed snake to emerge and start harassing me. Just the thought of her was enough to make my muscles tense up, but fear would do me no good. I had no time to waste. I needed the crystal and I needed it fast.

As I turned my head to stand up, something shiny in the field caught my eye, like a coin or maybe an Aphrodite quartz. I pounced on the glistening object feeling certain it was my crystal, but it squirmed in my fingers. Yuck! It was a humongous pink lightning bug. I hated all insects, even ladybugs and fireflies. Too creeped out to waste another minute resting, I dragged myself to a standing position and hobbled toward the empty carousel.

The more I thought about it the more I convinced myself that I must have dropped the crystal at the carousel. There really was no other place it could be—unless someone stole it.

Beautiful music, more like a symphony than the usual cheesy stuff you hear at a carnival, filled my ears. Soft at first, the music grew louder as I approached the platform. Someone had turned on the carousel. I hoped I'd see the horse and not a stranger. I held my breath. As the platform spun around, I could make out a white horse with gold-tipped hooves. Asca!

"I thought you'd come back," the horse said, his chin pressed against his chest. "You dropped this."

I hopped up onto the platform. The Aphrodite quartz peeked out from behind the horse's chin. "Thank you. You don't know what this means to me." I said, as Asea lifted his head and plopped the crystal into my palm.

"I'm afraid I do."

"When I go home, I'll use this crystal to find the secret notes or lure them to me or something. I'm not quite sure how it works."

"I understand why you're doing it. I know about your brother. I'd do the same thing if I were you, but please be careful."

"What do you mean?"

"The crystal stores energy but it also attracts

energy. The closer you get to finding the notes, the more dark energy you'll attract."

"I can't worry about dark energy," I replied. "I have to help my brother before it's too late."

"I remember a phrase Venusians used to repeat about the secret notes."

"What? What was it?"

Asea stared at the ground and then looked me in the eye.

"The secret notes are buried
But remain within the light."

"That doesn't rhyme," I insisted.

"I think there's another part with the color white," he added.

"So 'light' and 'white' are supposed to rhyme in the riddle?"

"I'm sorry I don't know the rest," the horse apologized, "but I know where your balloon is."

"You do? Did you see it land?"

"No. I didn't use my eyes—I used my mind," Asea blurted out. "Because there is awareness in everything, I aligned my mind with the balloon and waited for a signal. It's three fields over."

"Thank you. Thank you," I said almost singing with happiness.

Asea nodded. "Follow me."

The horse sprinted through the sunflower

field and I jogged behind. My legs were working much better now.

Approaching the hot air balloon, I noted that the balloon was inflated and ready for lift off as if I had ordered a taxi to take me to the airport. I dashed to the passenger basket and unlatched the door. Before stepping in, I triple-checked my right pocket to make sure the crystal was safely tucked away. It was. Then I climbed in and waved goodbye to the horse. I didn't have to fiddle with the controls to make the balloon work. I simply floated away.

Soaring higher and higher, I gazed down at the ground slipping away from me. From the air, fields of flowers hopscotched around the empty amusement park. I would miss the sights, the sounds, the air on Venus, but I needed to get home pronto. The image I saw in the library flipped my stomach upside down.

Feeling sleepy and mentally exhausted from the day, I rested my head on the floor of the basket. I kept thinking of Michael playing football with his friends. My eyelids, much too heavy to hold open, closed on their own.

Boom.

With a thud, I landed. I could hear the sounds of children laughing and country music playing. Groggy and confused, I battled to hold my drooping head up straight. It was the same disoriented feeling I had when I awoke from a cat nap in the afternoon. To keep my balance, I stood up slowly and clasped the side of the basket. About twenty feet away, the balloon man paced back and forth, chitchatting on his cell phone. He was supposed to meet his wife in town. Why was he still talking to her on the phone?

I took a moment to take in my surroundings, noting the sky was still bright with streaks of orange to the west. It was exactly the same scene I left before I traveled on the hot air balloon. Nothing had changed.

Wait! Did I dream up the trip to Venus? Did I drift off to sleep in the basket from sheer exhaustion? It was possible because ever since Michael's accident, I had trouble sleeping. Some nights I fell asleep quickly and then woke up after an hour or two, flipping back and forth in my bed until the early morning hours. Other nights I tossed in bed until one or two in the morning. I'm not sure I ever fell asleep on those nights.

If I did nod off in the basket, I couldn't have been sleeping more than five or ten minutes based on the position of the sun. It's funny how time stretches out in your dreams and then snaps back like a rubber band when you wake up.

The balloon man was still gabbing on his cell phone with his back to me, clueless that I had trespassed. Now was my chance to sneak out. No one was looking. I unlatched the door and took a step, but my legs were so numb, I nearly dropped to my knees.

It was as if my lower body belonged to someone else. I grasped the rim of the basket and waited for the blood to circulate through my veins. After a moment, I reclaimed my legs and stepped away from the balloon.

"I'm sorry you didn't get a ride today," the balloon man called out. I turned toward him and smiled, hoping my grin didn't reveal my secret.

"That's okay. I'll be back tomorrow," I answered.

"I'm looking forward to taking you up into the clouds. I promise you it's the ride of a lifetime."

"I'm sure it is. I can't wait."

I thought about everything I had experienced on Venus or rather in my dream of Venus. Never before had I awakened from such a vivid dream. Usually, I would jump out of bed with only sketchy images of a dream or nightmare. The sense of flying with birds. Or a bad guy in a cloak. Maybe someone died. I never could remember much after waking up—and that probably was a good thing. But now I could recall tiny details of the amusement park, the labyrinth, the Galactic Library. Plus all of the creatures I met—the three-headed snake, the talking horse, the statue girl. Celeste coming to life in the water fountain was carved in my mind as if it were true. The tingling smell of the roses and lilacs filled my nostrils even now. Absolutely nothing on Venus seemed like a dream. But it all must have been a dream because no time had passed while I was on the hot air balloon.

Baffled, I toddled through the field toward the other carnival rides, looking past the crowds and not at anyone in particular. I felt so dizzy, so groggy, like I had stepped off a wild roller coaster ride. But I hadn't—I was just napping in the passenger basket. Why couldn't I shake the woozy, heavy feeling cementing my feet to the ground? I had to snap out of it.

"Hey, Jack. Is that you?" a soft voice said from behind. I turned around and recognized Natalie Carter. She was good friends with Michael. They might have been friends since grade school. Maybe they were more than friends. I didn't really know because Michael never told me about his girlfriends. He always had girls calling him, texting him. I couldn't help but be envious.

"How's Michael doing? Does he recognize you yet?" Natalie asked.

"He still can't respond to anything. We don't know if he can hear us. My mom thinks he can, but I'm not so sure."

I was looking down at the pavement, shuffling my feet in the dirt. I couldn't wait to get away from Natalie. Most boys in my class would love to have the undivided attention of Natalie Carter, but not me. Or at least not on that day. I just couldn't talk about Michael to anyone. It hurt too much and I preferred to remain wrapped in my cocoon of grief. People of all ages paced around the grounds, laughing like everything was okay. But everything was not okay. Michael should have been with me and he wasn't.

"I gotta go, Natalie," I told her. "My mom will worry about me if I'm gone too long. I'll see you around." I slinked away feeling badly about lying to Natalie.

I was slowly making my way toward the exit, my legs feeling a little better with each step when someone tapped me on the shoulder. I must have jumped ten inches off the ground. "Here's your fish," a man said.

I spun around and recognized Chuck from the game booth. I had forgotten all about my goldfish prize. It seemed like days had passed since I played the fish game. Chuck reached out and handed me the fish bowl.

"Thanks for watching it."

"No problem. Send your friends to my booth tomorrow," he said.

"Sure," I muttered under my breath, knowing I wasn't going to be calling any friends. I didn't even want to face strangers.

With the fishbowl clutched in both hands, I sauntered home. The clouds in my head were lifting and I was steadier on my feet. Watching the goldfish glide through the water, I envied its carefree attitude.

Back and forth it swam. I named it Venus after my spectacular dream.

Turning onto my street, I gazed at my house for a moment. It wasn't a small house; it just seemed small since Michael's accident. There was nowhere to go to be alone, to clear my head, to breathe. Last spring, our house was painted lemon yellow with cornflower blue shutters. I helped my mom pick out the colors. But now the shades were pulled down and cobwebs stretched across the window frames. Weeds popped up from under the loose stones on the walkway. In all my life, I had never seen my house so neglected. In the span of only three weeks, everything had changed.

I opened the front door and slipped upstairs to my room, placing the fishbowl on my dresser. Then I tiptoed down the hall to Michael's room and peeked in. Michael looked like he was sleeping except for all the tubes plugged into his body. I touched him lightly on the wrist. "Michael, I'm sorry. I'm so sorry." He didn't move. I could feel stingy tears collecting behind my eyes. I turned and walked out.

My parents were in the kitchen and I didn't think they heard me come in. Like a small child awake way past bedtime, I perched myself on the third or fourth step and peered down at my parents. They were seated at the table with their backs to me. I couldn't tell if they were crying, but the air in the house gagged me. My mom buried her face in her left hand and stroked my dad's shoulder with her right. His shoulders twitched and he kept his hands clasped together under the table. His right foot tapped continuously on the floor.

I could tell from their body language that they had been fighting. My parents used to fight about money nearly every night after Michael and I went upstairs. My mom would start out speaking in a slow controlled voice that would escalate to a high-pitched screech. My father, always in control, wouldn't say much at first. He'd just pace the floor, sit down for a minute, and then jump up from the table and pace again. After about the third time he got up, he'd start hollering. Like a volcano spewing molten lava, there was no stopping him once he got started.

My parents didn't fight about money anymore. No one had mentioned money in three weeks. Now they argued about Michael. Should he go back to the hospital? Was he better off at home? But these arguments were just stand-ins for the real argument. The one nobody would dare utter out loud. Whose fault was it? Everyone knew where the blame belonged—on me, of course. I knew it and they knew it.

I could see my father getting more fidgety. He was twitching his shoulders like he had an itch, like he wanted to pull away from my mother. Without warning he pushed his chair back from the table and stood up in one explosive motion. "He has to go back to the hospital," my dad said.

"But I can take care of him. I'm his mother."

"What have you done for him? Nothing."

"I've tried to stimulate him," she offered.

"He's still a vegetable!" my dad snapped, his voice cracking on the word vegetable.

"Vegetative state does not mean vegetable. He's not a turnip, for God's sake," my mom said. Then she mumbled something else I couldn't make out.

"It doesn't matter what you call him. He's not waking up. He's got to go back to the hospital," my dad said, his shoes clacking against the kitchen floor.

"What does another couple of days matter? I think he knows me. He fluttered his eyes today. Let him stay home through the weekend. Do it for me."

"I listened to you and let the boys go to the shore. And look what happened. Tuesday morning he's going back under the doctor's care," my dad demanded. He never trusted my mom's medical knowledge because she wasn't a doctor. She was only a nurse. I always thought she knew as much as most of the doctors at the hospital.

For a moment, there was silence. I strained to listen but I could only hear my father's footsteps as he paced anxiously on the creaky wooden kitchen floor. I don't think he saw me peeking through the staircase spindles. My mother got up from the table and walked toward my dad. "George, my coma recovery support group thinks that—"

"Support group? How are they supporting us?" my dad mocked.

"They've suggested that I stimulate him and—"

"What a bunch of nonsense! You've had almost two weeks to stimulate him and nothing has changed. Maybe the real doctors can give him some drugs to stimulate him. I'm sick of all of your alternative medicine garbage. It doesn't work, Grace."

"Where are you going?" my mom asked.

"Out."

"Are you going to eat anything? I can make something."

"I'm not hungry," my dad answered. Then I heard the door close.

I wasn't hungry either. My appetite disappeared the day of the accident. I knew I was losing weight and should eat something, but I just couldn't. Even my favorite foods like pizza and ice cream didn't appeal to me. I could hear my mother scurrying in the kitchen opening and closing cabinets. Another door slammed shut.

My mom convinced the doctors at the hospital to discharge Michael after only ten days. She researched coma recovery and found medical cases where patients woke up from a coma after something called intense sensory stimulation. The day my brother arrived home she began her intense stimulation, never wavering in her commitment to the plan. In a journal, she recorded in detail each time she blasted music or shined a spotlight in his face. Her nonstop efforts would bring a dead person back to life. At least twice a day, my mom called me into my brother's room insisting that he was waking up from the coma. Some tiny part of me must have believed Michael could get better because every time my mom called for me, I sprinted into his room trusting he was waking up. Each time I ran into his room I was disappointed. She kept insisting he would regain consciousness one day. I kept believing her. My father, however, doubted Michael would ever improve. His oldest son, the athletic one just like him, remained lifeless, like a mannequin resting on the bed. That's all my dad could see, the frozen outer shell of his once perfect son.

I slipped back into my room, closed the door tightly, and sprawled my body across the twin mattress. Every muscle ached as if I had run a marathon, even though I'd never run more than two miles in my life. The sheets were bunched up in a ball at the bottom of the bed and the comforter lay in a heap on the floor. My bed hadn't been made in weeks. As I rested flat on my back, I could feel the tears welling up behind my eyeballs. I tried to think happy thoughts, but the images flew away. I would start sobbing soon if I didn't focus on something else.

I rolled over onto my stomach and smashed the pillow into my face. Something was jabbing my leg. I reached into my pocket and pulled out the pointy object.

The Aphrodite quartz! How could I have the Aphrodite quartz?

CHAPTER 6
Now What Do I do?

If I had the crystal, I couldn't have been dreaming about Venus. But if I weren't dreaming, how did I travel the millions of miles through space in zero time. How could this be true? Was I still dreaming? I pinched my wrist just to make sure I was awake. I was. I must have blasted through a hole in time and space on the hot air balloon. This seemed ridiculous, but there was no other explanation. I could feel my heart thumping against my ribs.

Clenching the crystal in my fist, I thought of the secret notes. Things seemed so clear on Venus but now I couldn't remember what I was supposed to do with the crystal. *Think hard*, I told myself staring up at the ceiling. Okay. What did the snake say? The silicon in the crystal held information about healing Michael. Or was the information in the secret notes? The girl at the fountain thought her brothers and sisters would be drawn to the crystal and they'd help me find the secret notes. But that could be a long shot.

I didn't know what was true and what wasn't. But I knew one thing for certain. The crystal guided me out of the glass labyrinth and got me home safely—so it definitely had some magical powers. I just had to figure out how to heal Michael with it. There had to be a way.

Images of Venus clicked through my head as if my mind were a digital camera. I remembered opening my book in the Galactic Library. More than any other scene, the image of Michael playing football in the backyard with his friends popped up over and over again. I froze that scene from the book in my head and locked my eyes on the purple light at the edge of the property line. Was I supposed to bury the crystal in my backyard? Could that be the answer?

I rolled the crystal between my fingers hoping it would send me a signal. The crystal felt intensely warm so I took that to mean that I was supposed to bury it. I decided I would sneak out of the house after my parents fell asleep and bury the Aphrodite quartz near Mr. Jenkins' cornfield.

"I'm home, Ma," I called out from the hallway. I could hear her shuffling in Michael's room, changing the blanket or fixing the bed.

"Want some dinner?" she asked.

"I ate at the carnival." The lie poured out of my mouth too easily.

I heard my father's heavy footsteps coming up the stairs. "Good night, Dad," I said from behind my closed door. I heard the door handle turn and then my father walked into my room. I could see his neck muscles bulging and his hand trembling.

"Good night, Jack," he said staring at me. I couldn't wait for him to walk out and close the door.

My parents watched TV in their room most evenings so there was no telling how long it would be before they turned out the lights. My mother couldn't sleep well before the accident. Now she didn't sleep at all or at least it seemed that way. No matter what hour of the night, I could hear her pacing the hallway or gently speaking to my brother. Every night, I wanted to jump out of bed and wrap my arms around her and cry and cry and cry until my face swelled up. But I never did. Instead, I stayed in my room with my door closed tightly, choking back the tears. I let her do all the crying. This evening she seemed particularly fidgety. I thought she'd never settle down and nod off. Hours passed before I felt certain they were both sleeping.

At precisely twelve twenty-two in the morning, with the house silent except for the ticking of my clock, I tiptoed downstairs and slipped out the kitchen door. A full moon bathed our backyard in light. I would not need a flashlight.

My mom kept her garden tools in a shed behind the garage. I wouldn't have any trouble finding a shovel because she owned at least ten in an assortment of sizes and colors. Heading toward the shed, I lifted my stinging eyes to the sky trying to remember where Venus was located. Before the accident, Michael and I sat on the front porch at night and searched for star constellations. He loved studying outer space as much as I did, but he would always let me peer through the telescope first. I could have asked for my own telescope at Christmas but I didn't need to put it on my list. Why waste money when Michael would share with me?

Quietly, I cracked open the shed door and retrieved a small shovel from my mother's collection. Now where to bury the crystal? I would have to dig a hole on our side of the property line. My whole life I had been careful not to trespass on Mr. Jenkins' fields because he could be kind of grumpy. My friends and I waited until we knew he wasn't home to retrieve any balls that rolled onto his property. Mr. Jenkins didn't want anyone trampling on his crops. I think he sold the corn at a local market and every ear of corn mattered to him. He never offered me any, but now even corn on the cob wouldn't tempt me.

With the crystal clasped in my right palm, I searched the edge of my yard for some kind of marking. I turned over rocks, pushed aside leaves and scrutinized every inch of soil. Finally, I settled on a spot just inches away from the cornfield, on my side of the property line. I pressed the end of the hand-held shovel into the ground but the soil was so dry I was barely able to dig up an inch of dirt. I tried again this time using both hands and throwing all of my weight against the shovel.

The sound of rustling in the bushes startled me. Was it a raccoon? A rabbit? I froze. I wasn't frightened up until that moment, but now I began to question my decision to come out alone in the middle of the night. I couldn't be certain but I thought I saw a snake squirm under the cornstalks. Then, all was quiet again.

Ignoring the pain in my blistered palms, I dug with every drop of strength I had until the hole was big enough to bury my hand. I placed the crystal in the middle and mouthed a silent prayer that Michael would wake up and everything would be okay. I scooped the earth up with my bare hands, covered the crystal, and then walked toward my house. Then I turned back. Was that really the right place to bury it?

I walked back to the mound of dirt and dug up the crystal. Something told me to plant the crystal in Mr. Jenkins' cornfield, in the spot where the football rolled. Maybe not such a great idea, but I would do it anyway.

Never looking up to see if anyone was watching me, I dug the hole, dropped the Aphrodite quartz into the dirt, and covered it up. Then I sprinted to my backdoor, hiding the shovel behind a flower pot. I creaked open the kitchen door and locked it behind me. My house was still quiet. There was a lightness in my footsteps, almost as if I were on Venus, as I tiptoed upstairs and washed my dirty hands in the bathroom sink. I crawled into bed with a smile on my face.

I am not certain I ever fell asleep, though. I might have been in that crazy place half way between asleep and awake when anything is possible.

Abruptly, a low crackling sound filled my ears. It sounded like it was coming from my backyard. I tilted open the wood blinds to take a peak quite certain I'd see something burning, even though I couldn't smell any smoke. The sizzling noise was getting louder and now a cone of pinkish-purple light seemed to be flowing out from the moon. The purple mist settled a few feet above the cornfields and twisted up and down like a funnel cloud. But here's the even stranger part: I wasn't scared. I felt exactly like I had felt when I landed on Venus, like a giant vacuum sucked all the pain out of my body. I pressed my nose against the window and watched as the purple mist danced above the field, spiraling down and then up again. Poof! It was gone.

I must have imagined the dancing purple mist, at least that's what I told myself over and over again as I kicked the sheets around in my bed. Still, something inside of me believed I had witnessed a real event in my backyard. Anxious to see if the purple mist had burned the ground or ruined the corn, I tossed in my bed for hours. I wanted to dash into the cornfield, but I thought I should wait until daylight. What if it happened again while I was outside?

At six in the morning, I bolted downstairs and ran into Mr. Jenkins' field unprepared for what stood before me. It was incredible! Sections of corn plants were pressed down—not broken, just gently bent, curving toward the earth in some type of pattern like a corn maze. I wished I could float in the hot air balloon above the field and snap a picture, but I couldn't so I did the next best thing. I strolled through the field careful not to crush the corn, following the twists in the path. What type of pattern was this and what did it mean? I stopped somewhere in the middle and detected the ground under my feet vibrating slightly as if an airplane were flying overhead. The corn stalks did not appear damaged. I peeled back the husk on an ear of corn to get a better look. I don't know if I expected the kernels to glow or have changed color, but they looked perfectly normal to me. I continued on the path.

In less than ten minutes, I found myself back at the starting point on the edge of my property. The pattern in the field was not a maze but a labyrinth, just as I had seen on Venus. I took that as a sign that burying the crystal had worked. Michael would be coming out of the coma soon. I skipped back into my house, my heart bursting.

I climbed the stairs and proceeded directly into Michael's room, as if he would be sitting up in bed waiting for me. He wasn't. Gazing at my brother's limp, lifeless body, I wished I could switch places with him. "Michael, I'm so sorry," I whispered over and over, grasping his clammy hand. He didn't move. He remained stiff and silent like a corpse. The artificial ventilator made the only sound in his room.

"Michael, you're going to wake up. I planted the crystal in the ground. It's all charged up and ready to activate your DNA. You'll wake up soon."

No response.

Even though there had been no visible change in his condition, I felt certain Michael would come out of the coma. Otherwise, why would the purple mist have formed a labyrinth in Mr. Jenkins' cornfield? It was only a matter of time before Michael hopped out of bed and greeted me.

I bounded down the stairs to the kitchen to prepare a feast forgetting there wasn't much food in the house. My mother hadn't purchased more than the bare essentials at the grocery store in weeks.

Rummaging through the fridge, I found two eggs behind a plastic container of what might have been coleslaw. After frying the eggs, I sat at the kitchen table and stared out the sliding glass door at the cornfield.

My shoulders tensed up as I noticed two men in dark clothing examining the corn stalks, but I couldn't make out their faces. The taller man turned and pointed at me or rather at my house but it seemed like he was pointing at me. The other man took a few steps into my yard but then turned back toward the corn. I wondered if they knew about the crystal or if Mr. Jenkins had hired them to investigate the strange occurrence in his field. I wasn't sure if I knew what happened. Had I dreamed up the whole thing? I decided not to tell my parents about my trip to Venus, the crystal, or the purple mist. I could have told my mother. She would have listened without laughing at me. Maybe I could have told my father. Maybe not. I would keep everything a secret at least for the time being, especially since the two men didn't look friendly.

CHAPTER 7
Alone

Beeep! Beeep! The bedside alarm blasted in Michael's room. I could hear my parents shouting and the sound of feet scurrying across the floorboards above me. I sprinted up the stairs into my brother's room.

"What happened?" I blurted out.

"He's not getting enough oxygen," my mom shrieked, her fingers trembling as she pushed buttons on the ventilator. "Call an ambulance!"

I ran to the phone in my parents' room and dialed 911. The operator said they'd be at my house in less than three minutes. "They're coming, Ma!" I yelled out and ran back to Michael's room.

My father stood at Michael's bedside, both of their faces paper white.

"The doctors warned that this could happen," my mom mumbled. She was shaking her head back and forth. "I think he's inhaling a little more oxygen now, but it won't last."

"Why can't he get enough oxygen?" I questioned. It didn't make any sense. Michael was still hooked up to a ventilator.

"There must be fluid in his lungs. He might have pneumonia." Tears were collecting in the corners of her eyes but she was trying to appear brave.

"How would he get pneumonia?"

"Reflux from his feeding tube," my mom said in her nurse voice. "Even though he can't eat, the goop can get stuck in his lungs."

I could hear the siren from a few blocks away. As it got louder and louder, a sense of relief passed through me.

Three EMS workers barged in the front door and ran up the steps. They scampered around his bed pressing buttons on the ventilator just as my mother had done.

"I think he's stabilized," one of the emergency workers said.

"Can you help me lift him onto the stretcher, Crystal?" a dark-haired man with glasses asked.

Crystal? How strange that the woman's name was Crystal!

The team of EMS workers spent a minute or two checking Michael's vital signs. Then they connected him to a portable ventilator, placed him on a stretcher, and carried him down the stairs. My knees weak, I trailed my parents down the steps grabbing the handrail.

"Can I go with you?" I asked. I knew there wasn't anything I could do to help Michael at the hospital but I just wanted to be with him.

"You can't come to the hospital. Michael will be in the intensive care unit for a while," my mom explained. "They won't let children under sixteen into the room. We'll let you know how he's doing."

I let out a puff of air. There was no sense in arguing with her—she knew hospitals well. Besides, I didn't think my parents needed any more stress from me.

A moment later everyone scrambled out the front door. Alone with my thoughts, the silence picking at my head, I couldn't help but wonder if there were some connection between the buried crystal and Michael's condition. The purple mist should have healed Michael, not made things worse! What did I do? Maybe I didn't bury the crystal in the right place. Or maybe I just had to be more patient. The secret notes would show up. My head felt so heavy I could have collapsed in the foyer.

I don't think I was alone in the house fifteen minutes when the front doorbell rang, not once but three times. Normally, I wouldn't have answered the door, but I thought it might be a medical worker getting something for my brother. I peeked through the glass peephole to get a better look. I could see a police officer with a clipboard in his hand talking to someone else. I started to open the door without undoing the chain. Through the crack between the door and the frame I saw Mr. Jenkins and another policeman. My heart sank to my knees.

"Are your parents home?" the shorter policeman asked.

"No, Sir. They're at the hospital with my

brother," I answered.

"Were you in this man's cornfield last night?"

"No."

"Was your brother?"

"No. He's in the hospital in a coma," I mumbled.

"We think you're lying to us. We have proof you were in the field." He drew in a deep breath and slowly exhaled. "Charlie here saw you walking on his property this morning and he took a picture."

I got a good look at the other policeman, the taller one who hadn't uttered a word. I almost wished I hadn't. His face was hideous, with large pock marks clumped together across his cheeks and jaw. His skin was a sickly greenish-white. But his eyes, they were the scariest part of his face. Two large yellowed eyeballs bulged out of the sockets as if he had no eyelids. "I'm Officer Danson and this is Officer Smith," the creepy policeman said in a deep voice. "I think you know your neighbor, Mr. Jenkins."

I nodded my head but said nothing. It wasn't his words that rattled me, it was his tone. Danson continued, "We think you and some of your buddies were real comedians last night. You thought it would be funny to make a crop circle in your neighbor's cornfield."

"What's a crop circle?" I asked, although I could almost guess the answer.

"A crop circle is a prank. It's where spoiled

kids think they're real funny so they chop down crops and make a design in the field."

"Why would someone do that?" I questioned.

"So people will think aliens have invaded. Did you think you were funny last night?" Danson asked, with a cocky grin.

"No. I didn't do anything."

"Why were you in the field this morning?" Danson asked, shoving his face into the crack between the door and the frame.

I jumped back. "I-I-I didn't do anything wrong." I tried to shut the door, but his foot was propping it open.

"Why is there dirt under your fingernails?"

"I didn't do anything wrong," I repeated, twisting my hand to see the dirt.

"Where'd you get those blisters?"

"I did nothing."

"You trespassed and vandalized property. You need to come down to the station for questioning," Danson said, pointing his finger at my face.

"I can't."

"Get your parents. You're coming with us."

"But my parents aren't home."

Smith whispered something to Danson and then said out loud, "Okay. You'll come down later when they come back."

Danson wasn't giving up so easily. He

seemed determined to get me to admit to something. "What did you use to chop down the corn stalks?" he asked.

"Nothing. I didn't do it." I was visibly shaking but the cops showed no mercy.

"We have a warrant to search your property. We want to know what type of device you used. Hand it over or we'll turn this place into a junk yard."

"I have nothing."

"But you did have something, didn't you?"

"No. I didn't do anything. I—"

Danson cut me off. "Fine, we're going to search your property."

Through the crack in the door, I watched all three men storm off. I slammed the door shut and bolted it. Then I ran to the kitchen and flattened my body against the back wall so I could see out the sliding glass door, hoping they couldn't see me. They were headed for the shed. What did they think they would find? A giant rolling pin?

Pressed against the kitchen wall, I continued to study their every move. Danson turned and faced my house, giving my mother's vegetable garden a sidelong glance. His eyes lingered on the spot in my yard where I first buried the crystal. Did he think the crystal was still there? I wouldn't let him or the others know I was watching. They might think I was guilty if they saw me gawking at them.

Smith and Mr. Jenkins left my property and

stepped into the cornfield, but Danson lagged behind. He said something to the others I couldn't hear and then wandered toward my house. As he approached, his bug eyes darted back and forth, jiggling in their sockets, igniting a fear deep inside me. Something about this cop disturbed me but I couldn't identify exactly what. From every bone in my body, I sensed he knew about the crystal. I ran through a scenario in my mind. Maybe he was patrolling the streets in the middle of the night and saw me bury the crystal in the cornfield. He didn't need to shine a flashlight because the full moon lit my backyard like a spotlight. It was possible. Doubtful, but still possible. My heart thumped against my rib cage as I watched him examine my yard. I wouldn't let him take the crystal.

The distant sound of sirens grew louder, reminding me of Michael. It couldn't be my brother, though. He was already at the hospital. I closed my eyes, sucked in shallow breaths, and exhaled through my mouth, praying for Michael's safe return home. When I opened my eyes, I saw the two cops dashing across my lawn toward the squad car. Mr. Jenkins was nowhere to be seen. As the blare of the siren faded in the distance, I took deeper and deeper breaths. They were gone.

By now it was 9:30 in the morning. The fried eggs I had been so excited to eat lay untouched on my plate. My stomach, twirling in knots, ached like I had the stomach flu. I simply did not know what to do. It seemed no matter what I did, no matter how good my intentions were, I inflicted pain on everyone—my brother, my parents, even Mr. Jenkins. A black, dense cloud shadowed my every move. I must have done something wrong—something terribly wrong. All I could think of was the hideous three-headed snake. She was using me—getting me to transport the Aphrodite quartz to earth. I was a fool to believe her. Why did I trust a snake?

The many conversations I had on Venus with the horse, Celeste, and Fagan replayed in my mind. Nobody thought searching for the secret notes was a good idea. I couldn't say they didn't warn me because they did. But I felt so safe with the crystal—like nothing could hurt me. How could I be so dumb?

And then it hit me! Of course. The crystal was still contaminated with snake energy. Celeste said I had to balance it in the four elements. I didn't listen to her and look what happened. If I could figure out how to balance the crystal in the four elements, everything would be perfect. I would cure Michael.

Okay. I needed a plan. Easier said than done. I could stay cooped up in my house all day, waiting for my parents to come home. What if the cops returned? What if they smashed in the front door and dragged me to the police station? Not a good option. I could also go to the carnival and spend the day meandering through the crowds and wasting time on rides. That seemed pointless. Deep within me, I knew what I wanted, what I needed—to return to Venus and the Galactic Library. If I got a chance to look at my book again I wouldn't foolishly run out the door. I'd study every page until I knew exactly what to do. I would figure out where the secret notes were. I knew I would. Just seeing that image of Michael playing football with his friends made me believe it was possible. The purple mist had something to do with it, but I needed more information, much more information. The first step was sneaking back onto the hot air balloon.

CHAPTER 8
The Haunted Maze

I ran upstairs to get money and was sickened to see my poor fish floating at the top of his bowl. Dead in less than 24 hours.

Clutching the bowl in both hands, I walked to the bathroom down the hall and promptly flushed Venus down the toilet. Then I wrote my parents a note saying I'd be back before dark.

When I stepped outside, a feeling of dread settled at the bottom of my stomach. I was sure the cops had left, but I felt like I was being stalked. If Mr. Jenkins saw me digging in his yard, he would have me hauled off to jail. That would be his proof. Still, I had to retrieve the crystal before Danson got his hands on it. The Aphrodite quartz was rightfully mine.

I couldn't risk being seen going back to the shed for a shovel. Instead, I walked directly to my property line, to the edge of Mr. Jenkins' cornfield, to look for witnesses. Glancing to the left and then to the right, I detected no one. Fortunately, I had no trouble locating the spot where I buried the crystal because the earth was darker in that area of the field. Using only my hands, I pushed away the loose dirt covering the Aphrodite quartz and plopped it in my right pocket. I liked the way the crystal felt in my pocket, not like a lump of change more like a lucky charm.

The first thing I did when I reached the carnival grounds was run up to the balloon launch site, but the man and his balloon weren't there. In fact, there was no trace of anything and I began to think I had imagined the entire trip to Venus. Where could the balloon be? I checked back every half hour, disappointed to see nothing, my heart sinking further as the day wore on. I couldn't give up hope yet. I didn't want to go back home and face Mr. Jenkins and the cops. I would continue strolling around the carnival, hoping the balloon would show up soon.

Nothing about the rides and games thrilled me anymore. I just felt lost. Several times I bumped into someone I knew, but I managed to avoid saying much about Michael. Other times, I ducked down or turned away especially when I saw one of Michael's teammates. The football players practiced most afternoons in the field directly in front of my house, but I couldn't bear to watch them play ball. Michael used to practice with them. He was so excited to play on the junior varsity team this year. That was all he ever talked about. Not anymore.

There was something about facing his friends that unnerved me. For years, I pretended to be proud of Michael and all of his trophies. My big brother the jock. Who wouldn't be happy for their older brother? A normal kid would beam with pride, right? But I wasn't a normal kid. I had a secret. The kind of secret that festers like an oozing blister under a Band-Aid. I could barely admit the secret to myself. Sometimes in the deepest, darkest part of the night, the truth gurgled to the surface. Although I loved my brother, I was so envious of him. Did my bottled up negative feelings cause the accident? Deep inside every cell in my body was the truth—the accident was my fault. One-hundred percent my fault. I had to get back on the balloon and make everything right again.

Noticing a sign with the words "Haunted Maze of Madness", I stopped and took note of the new attraction. The air felt different in front of this ride, thicker, heavier. I didn't recognize the haunted maze from other years, not that I knew every ride, but I had tried most of them. I would have expected a long line of kids circling around the back. Haunted houses were usually so popular. I wondered if the Haunted Maze had closed for the day. My question was answered when an intimidating man with a jagged scar on his chin emerged from behind a black, wooden door. It wasn't his body size that bothered me because he was rather small for a grown man—it was the intensity in his eyes, his glare. With a pitted face and twisted bony fingers he appeared cartoonish. He wore a wrinkled red t-shirt with something written in small white letters, something I couldn't make out. His snakeskin pointy boots looked brand new, but his jeans were tattered. His silver hair was pulled back neatly in a pony tail as if he made one gesture to appear presentable before leaving for work.

"Would you like to come inside? I can't promise you'll ever come out though," the man cackled.

It was just a game. He was trying to scare kids to make the haunted maze seem more frightening. That was his job but I could never understand why people would pay to get scared.

"I'm out of tickets," I told him. I lied. Of course I had more tickets. I turned back toward the Ferris wheel.

"Try out my maze unless you're a little baby—too scared to go on the big kid rides," he taunted.

"I'm not afraid. I know it's a big joke. You're just some guy getting paid to frighten kids," I said, with my back to him.

"If you're not chicken, come in."

"No thanks."

As I started to walk away, I noticed football players approaching me. Did they see me? I didn't think so, but I couldn't be sure. The kids laughed and hollered like nothing had changed—like Michael was still there. The football players were getting closer, now only a few feet away. I couldn't look at them. I had to hide. I didn't want to talk to people—especially Michael's teammates. The guilt gnawed at me. At any cost, I avoided people who might ask questions, who might make me feel worse than I already did. I decided to slip into the "Haunted Maze of Madness" rather than face Michael's friends.

"Tickets. I need four tickets from each of you," the ride attendant said, tapping the arm of a girl in a striped blue rugby shirt. I didn't recognize her.

I fumbled in my left pocket and pulled out a fist of tickets. The Aphrodite quartz remained safe in the other pocket. I held the four tickets out without making eye contact with the carnival guy, but he didn't take them so I stuffed them back in my pocket.

"I knew you'd return," he snickered.

I didn't respond. Instead I followed the group of kids directly ahead of me, keeping my face within two inches of the girl in the blue shirt. I couldn't see much, just a thin cone of red light projecting up from a crack in the floorboards.

As we walked further and further into the maze, my eyes adjusted to the dim lighting. The haunted house appeared as if someone constructed it in a hurry, a last-minute rush job. Painted masks about two feet apart hung in mid-air. No bodies, no voices, just masks with glowing eyes. The eyes seemed to follow me and I couldn't shake the feeling I was being watched. Pipe organ music filled the room but I couldn't see any speakers. I wasn't frightened by the makeshift haunted house, just anxious to find the exit. I felt certain the football players had passed the entrance and now I wished I could just find my way out. Haunted houses were so stupid.

Then something tripped me.

A rock? An uneven floorboard? A foot? I crashed to the ground, using my hands to break my fall as well as the backs of a few kids in front of me. My heart jittered with the sound of something hard clanking against the concrete. Did the crystal fall out of my pocket? I would never find it in the darkness if it did. I just couldn't lose the crystal.

Holding my breath, I dragged my fingers across my pocket. The lump was still there. I jammed my hand into my jeans and felt the smooth texture and warmth of the Aphrodite quartz. I exhaled.

As I labored to stand up, someone shoved me from behind. With everyone pressed together, I couldn't be sure whether the person had pushed me on purpose or not. Must be part of the act.

"I think you owe me something," the creepy carnival guy whispered, kneeling down behind me. His hot, dragon breath on the back of my neck unnerved me.

"What?" I mumbled as I got back on my feet. *It's just a carnival ride*, I told myself but somehow I knew it was more than that.

"You didn't pay me for the ride."

"Here," I said, shoving the four tickets in his face.

"I don't want those tickets."

"You said the ride costs four tickets," I insisted, my voice strengthening with each word.

"Empty your pockets. I'll see what you have of value."

"No. I'm not emptying my pockets. I offered you the tickets and you refused to take them."

"I have enough tickets. I'd like something else. Let me see what you've got."

"Nothing," I stated with confidence. I had no idea where it came from.

"Then give me the tickets," he demanded.

I fished out the tickets and held them over my shoulder. He snatched them out of my hand and hissed. Throngs of kids pressed against me from all sides, but rather than be annoyed I was comforted by their presence. I didn't realize there were so many kids inside the haunted house when I entered it. At least I wasn't alone.

I nestled my body between the girl in the blue shirt and the tall kid in a baseball cap. As we continued traipsing through the maze, I kept my line of vision glued to the backs of the kids in front of me. I could feel the dangling masks glare at me, but as the organ music grew softer, I knew I was getting closer to daylight. And then, finally, the glorious red exit sign appeared.

As I walked out, I turned back to see if the carnival guy was stalking me. I could find no sign of him. He must be on a break or maybe he was terrorizing some other poor kid. Was it possible he knew about the crystal? No. How could he? The Haunted Maze was just a carnival ride, nothing else. I needed to remain focused on my goal: sneaking back on the hot air balloon.

As the day advanced toward nightfall, my restless spirit grew angry. Where was the balloon? Again and again, I returned to the launch site but was disappointed to see nobody there. The yellow chaser truck was gone as well as the giant inflating apparatus. The only thing that suggested I hadn't dreamed up the hot air balloon was the pressed down patch of grass where the balloon was anchored. What if I couldn't go back to Venus? I trudged back toward the other rides.

"Would you like to have a go at the gopher?" a carnival worker asked as I slid by him. "Yes, I'm asking you."

"I'm out of money," I answered, patting my pockets.

"The first game's on me. I haven't had too many customers today. I'm bored. Grab the mallet and whack as many gophers as you can in thirty seconds."

"How many do I have to smack?" I asked, tempted to try. Something about smashing the mallet against plastic gophers appealed to me.

"Let's say if you hit fifteen, you can play again."

"Fair enough," I said, squeezing the mallet in my right fist. As gophers popped up from six different holes, I'd have to smack them down before they dropped out of sight. Simple enough.

I pounded the first gopher and then the second, feeling my boiling blood zoom through the veins in my forearm. Gophers kept popping up and I kept smacking them down. When the end buzzer sounded, I felt like I was on another planet.

"Twenty-two gophers!" the carnival man called out. "I don't think I've ever seen anyone hit so many in a row. That's got to be a record. Play again. I promised you another game."

And so I did. I lost track of time smashing the gophers. I played and played until another kid tapped me on the shoulder wanting a turn. I spun around and recognized his barbecue-chip colored hair before I got a good look at his face. It was Bradley from the Ferris wheel. I slipped my right hand into my pocket and stroked the Aphrodite quartz.

"I never got a chance to look at your magic rock," I said.

"I don't have it anymore," Bradley muttered under his breath.

"What? Where is it?" my heart sank in disappointment.

"A policeman told me I had to give it to him. I didn't want to."

"So why did you?"

110

"He said I could ride in his car with the siren on if I gave it to him."

"What did the policeman look like?" I asked, guessing what he'd say.

"He looked yucky like a Halloween mask," Bradley replied. He handed the carnival man a ticket and took a turn whacking the gophers.

I thought about Officer Danson. He had to be the policeman who sweet-talked the crystal out of Bradley. Danson wanted my crystal and he wanted Bradley's because they were twin crystals. But how would he know that? Now he had Bradley's crystal, but he wanted mine too. One crystal was not enough for him. He needed both. But why? Maybe I needed both. Maybe Michael didn't wake up from the coma after I buried the crystal because I had only half of the puzzle. The one thing I knew for certain was that I had to get back to Venus and the Galactic Library.

"When did you give your magic rock to the policeman?" I asked after Bradley finished smashing gophers.

"A little while ago."

"This morning?"

"Yeah."

"Where's your mom?" I asked, wondering if she could answer a few questions about Danson.

"My mom isn't here. She's at the hospital having a baby."

"You're alone?"

111

"My nanny is over there holding my balloons."

"Where did you give the policeman your magic rock? Here at the carnival?" I asked.

"No. At my house when he came to take my mom to the hospital."

"But how did he know you had a magic rock?"

"He saw the beautiful colors in my fishbowl. He asked if I had any cool rocks to put in the bowl." Bradley looked down at the pavement. "I showed him my purple rock and he said he wanted it."

"I don't think I would take a ride in his squad car if I were you. You can't trust that policeman."

"But he's a policeman," Bradley insisted. "He's a good guy."

"I don't think so," I said under my breath.

Bradley's nanny waved him over before I had a chance to say goodbye. I walked away, now more confused than ever. If the crystals contained infinite power, then Danson must have planned to use the crystals for something. But what? Did he need both of them or only one?

Sometime in the late afternoon, maybe four or five o'clock, I noticed the hot air balloon lying flat in the field. I could see the yellow chaser truck barreling toward the launch site. When the truck came to a stop, the balloon man stepped out of the passenger side and approached me.

"Fagan?" I whispered just to see if he'd respond to the name.

"What?" the balloon man asked.

"It's just that you look like someone I know."

"I thought you'd be back this morning," the balloon man said with a disappointed look on his face. "Where were you?"

"I couldn't make it because my brother had to go back to the hospital."

"Is he okay?"

"I don't know. I'm not old enough to visit the intensive care unit."

"It's just as well that you didn't come this morning. The balloon envelope ripped on a branch coming down. We had quite a tough time mending it."

"Are you going up this evening?" I piped up.

"We won't be able to fly until tomorrow morning at 7 am."

"Why not?"

"I don't have enough propane in the burners. I'm just going through a test phase right now. You can watch," the balloon man offered.

Every bone and every muscle in my body felt lighter as if I were already on Venus. I merely had to sneak onto the balloon when no one was looking and I'd be on my way back. I still wasn't sure how to operate it, but if I pushed and pulled enough knobs

I'd get the balloon in the air. I shoved my hand in my pocket to check for the crystal. My Aphrodite quartz was tucked away safely.

"Are you going to inflate it now?" I asked, hoping he'd say yes.

"Yep. Why don't you help me?"

Together we spent twenty minutes blowing up the balloon with cold air. After the balloon was more than half-way inflated, the balloon man connected it to the basket and fired up the burners.

"Are you going to test it now?" I asked.

"In a minute. I have to make a phone call. Wait here."

I eyed the balloon man as he walked away. *Don't turn around*, I mentally told him. Quickly, I wrenched open the basket door, hopped in and ducked out of sight. None of the red and blue knobs on the control panel looked like the "on" switch. I had accidentally done it once before, I'd do it again. Which one could it be? Closing my eyes, I created a mental image of Venus—the amusement park, the Galactic Library—but the images evaporated in my mind. The truth was I was scared. What if the tear in the balloon ripped open again while I floated in the atmosphere? Not good. What if I got to Venus but I couldn't return to the Galactic Library? I started doubting myself, as usual.

When I opened my eyes, I randomly pulled a lever in the middle of the panel and started floating upward immediately, slowly and peacefully at first. The tranquil feeling didn't last long. As I drifted in the balloon basket, I knew that something had changed. Something had gone terribly wrong!

CHAPTER 9
Where Am I?

The first thing I noticed was the sky. Only a few minutes before, the sun was shining, circling the clouds with a radiant glow. Now the sky appeared a strange shade of moldy gray. The gentle breeze transformed into a cold, howling wind that would cut the skin off me. I just couldn't squash the fear that something was terribly wrong.

Shivering with the dropping temperature, I crouched down in the basket to shield my face from the whipping wind. I squeezed my eyes shut and tried to imagine the beautiful Venus I visited only a day before, but the fleeting image slipped away. A putrid odor was filling my nostrils and making my head spin. I opened my eyes and peered over the basket to see what was causing the stench. There were no factories or refineries to explain the nauseating odor, but I couldn't really see much because the sky was thickening like stew. Why was the atmosphere so dense? Was I traveling to the Venus we see from earth? …The Venus with a thick cloud of poisonous gas that would suffocate a human in two seconds flat? I made a terrible mistake.

My lungs grew heavy, like I was buried in sand with nothing but a thin straw connecting me to the air above. When I was eight or nine years old, Michael and his friends buried me in the sand at the

116

beach. It was just for fun. Although I wore a snorkel mask, the heavy sand pressed down on my chest, restricting my breathing to the point where I nearly suffocated. I couldn't get up and tell them to stop. That suffocating sensation again. My mind drifted...

With a jolt, the balloon started dropping. I glanced up at the balloon trying to determine if the section that the balloon man patched ripped open again. I could see black threads dangling from the inside of the balloon. My heart jack hammered in my chest. And then, without warning, the flame from the burners blew out, but I didn't touch any knobs. I swear I didn't.

How could I land when the air was choking me? Somehow I must have become trapped in the old Venus—the one before the Great Transition. How much longer did I have before the atmosphere on Venus cremated me?

I reached into my pocket and clutched my Aphrodite quartz crystal. I fought to hold a positive picture in my mind, but negative thoughts consumed me, shackled me. Goosebumps covered my arms and the back of my neck and I couldn't stop quivering.

By now, a greenish soupy fog completely obstructed my view. Still, I sensed the balloon would land within a minute or two because I had been dropping for some time. I sat down on the floor of the basket, pressed my back against the side, and covered my head, bracing myself for the crash. I imagined the gaping hole in the balloon growing in size. Thoughts of my brother, my parents, and friends whirled in my mind. How would my parents cope with both my death and my brother's condition? It was my fault for getting on the stupid balloon. Now I had made things much, much worse.

Thump!

The balloon smashed into the ground. Not the soft landing I had enjoyed the first time I visited Venus. With the thick greenish fog surrounding me, I couldn't see my hands or feet. I really couldn't make out anything. How was I breathing? How was I still alive? I thought that the basket splintered into pieces, but I couldn't see enough to confirm it. How would I ever get home now? I struggled to suck in the thick, dank air with rapid, shallow breaths. A foul metallic taste lingered on my tongue. Somehow, I had to find Asea or Celeste.

I groped the basket door and unlocked the latch. Then, I pushed the door open and stumbled out, tripping and landing in what I believed to be a prickly bush. I rolled out of the bush onto the cold, damp ground. Wearing only a short-sleeved shirt and blue jeans, I fought to stay warm by pulling my knees close to my chest.

My stinging eyes were adjusting to the darkness and now I could make out shadows. I should have cried. A normal kid would have cried. But I didn't. Somehow, my face remained frozen, with my body balled up, rocking back and forth.

A hissing, buzzing sound nudged me out of the trance. What was that? I felt distinct movement on my arms and legs—I definitely was not imagining things. Soon, a slight tickling sensation escalated to a pinching. Something was crawling all over me or, rather, thousands of creepy things were crawling all over my body, nipping me. The prickly bush must have been a nest of insects. Bugs marched across my face, down my neck and under my shirt. Each one feasted on my flesh as if I were a rotting corpse. The incredible itching and stinging was too much to bear. I screamed, jumping up and shaking my arms and legs. I tugged at the bugs, trying to pull them off of me, but it didn't help. Instead, more and more bugs crawled up and down my body, sticking to my clammy skin and gnawing me. Then, the buzzing sound got louder and louder and I could feel bugs scampering in my ear canal. I jammed my finger in my ear and tried to yank them out, but I pushed them in further. I screamed for help but only the howling wind answered my call. Then, I remembered my crystal.

I clasped the Aphrodite quartz between my fingers and gently hummed. I don't know why I started humming, but as I did, the insects lifted off my skin and melodically hummed along with me. Next, they appeared to swoosh together in a black funnel cloud and fly away. I couldn't see where they went but their humming grew softer and softer. They were gone!

I took as deep of a breath as I could muster, pulling the air through my nose. The stench remained, but it didn't seem as bad. Maybe the air improved or maybe I had just gotten used to it.

With the fog thinning, I now could see ten to fifteen feet in front of me. This was a mucky swamp with tufts of high grass scattered between rocks and decaying tree stumps. It could be the dark, shadow side of Venus, if such a place existed. I recalled what Asea had said about my fears coming true if I didn't control my thoughts. *Be positive*, I told myself. I longed to hop back into the balloon and return to the Labor Day carnival.

I squeezed my eyes shut and stepped back toward the balloon. I tried to imagine the balloon in perfect condition waiting to take me home. But when I opened my eyes, the balloon lay in ruins. The wicker basket had snapped in at least three places. I'd never get home now. Fighting back the tears, I surveyed my surroundings. How far was I from the amusement park?

Promptly, a flicker of light appeared about fifteen feet in front of me, beckoning in the thin fog. "Asea! Asea!" I called out, cupping my hands around my mouth.

No reply.

"Asea, are you here?"

No reply.

I hiked through the marsh toward the dim light, trusting that a Venusian would appear to help me. Somewhere behind me, I heard muffled footsteps, the crackling of twigs and the swishing of fabric against branches. I spun around but couldn't see anyone.

"Who's there?" I whispered, clasping my crystal. No one answered. I just couldn't shake the feeling that someone or something was following me. It was the same feeling I had in the Haunted Maze at the carnival. I stopped and glanced quickly from side to side. From out of the corner of my right eye, I thought I saw a moving figure. My heart raced as a burst of energy pulsed though my veins. I ran toward the light huffing and puffing, my lungs burning for more oxygen. My feet kept getting stuck in the mud, but I didn't stop. I ran and ran trying to outpace the stalker. The flickering light never got any closer, but the stalker never reached me either.

After a short while, I couldn't run anymore. Panting with my head spinning, I stopped near a large, stone object. I collapsed onto the mucky ground and tried to imagine that everything was a dream. Lying on my back with my chin tilted up, I pinched my eyes shut, placing my fingers in my pant pocket and stroking my crystal. Somehow, someway, I was going to get out of there.

When I finally felt stronger, braver, and

calmer, I stood up. It appeared I had been on the ground for hours judging by the change in the sky. The green fog had lifted and a glimmer of light peeked through the remaining thin layer of fog. Where was I?

Blinking a few times, I could now make out amusement park rides, but they were not the same ones I saw the first time I visited Venus. They appeared rusty and dilapidated—like they hadn't been used in over a hundred years. I must have landed in a different section of the amusement park.

Passing a rickety roller coaster, I noticed a carousel tucked behind it. While I still couldn't see much in the distance, I could have sworn I saw horses on the platform. Maybe Asea was there. Yes. He had to be there. My heart quickened as I sprinted toward the merry-go-round.

"Asea, is that you?" I asked, now only feet away.

No response.

"Asea! Asea!" I called out.

None of the horses moved. I could see that their coats were filthy gray and their tails were clumped in knots. Tarnished brass poles pierced their backs. Where you would expect to see a saddle, each horse had a blob of dingy hair. There was no music, just the whistling sound of the wind. I shuddered partly because I was cold but mostly because I was scared out of my mind.

Reaching into my pocket, I stroked the crystal. I wouldn't lift my fingers off the crystal. I had nothing else. My balloon lay in shambles and I was all alone. (That was assuming the stalker didn't return.) I kept shuffling through the park, holding onto the glimmer of hope that Asea would appear. Maybe I'd wander to Celeste's fountain. Could I get that lucky?

After walking in circles for quite some time, I stumbled upon an ornate bridge that seemed to appear out of nowhere. Maybe it crossed to the other section of the amusement park. Yes. That had to be it.

Stopping in front of the bridge, I sucked in as much air as my lungs could possibly hold and then exhaled slowly. I felt certain my Venusian friends waited for me on the other side.

Directly in front of the bridge stood two marble statues. I stepped closer to examine them. The carved sculptures appeared lifelike, but not lifelike in a human way—more like gargoyles in medieval stories. Their tails and wings were partially tucked in, as if they were surrendering to a beating. Both statues displayed fangs and claws, yet I couldn't imagine either one attacking another creature. An expression of profound sadness was carved in the face of the gargoyle positioned on the right. With down-turned lips and half-closed eyes, it reminded me of a child whose cherished pet had just died. Not a pet like a fish, more like a dog or cat. The left-hand gargoyle appeared more stunned than depressed with shock chiseled onto its stone face, like someone caught off-guard.

"We're not as pitiful as you think," the gargoyle on the left blurted out of his granite mouth.

"Who are you?" I asked, glaring at the frightened stone figure.

"My name is Puck and that's my twin sister, Portia." The creature gestured clumsily with his bird wing.

As Puck spoke, both stone creatures morphed into living mythological beings, just as Celeste had done at the water fountain. I noted that their wings were deformed, as if chopped by an axe. Both of the twins had lion faces with flickering violet-red slit eyes and plush, chocolate brown manes. Their lower bodies were scaly and reptilian, like a crocodile's. The twins stood on their hind lion legs, but not erectly, more like hunched old people. I chuckled, imagining a child combining mismatched puzzle pieces to design these creatures. I didn't want to let either one of them see me laugh.

"What are you?" I asked.

"We are Venugans, part lion and part lizard with useless wings," Puck said. "We originally come from Venus."

"What do you mean originally? Where are we now?"

"We're on Pluto, the most forsaken planet in

the universe," Puck answered, looking away.

"Pluto? Pluto the planet?"

"Yes."

I was sure Puck and Portia could hear my heart beating in my chest. Portia remained silent, never taking her flashing eyes off of me. I didn't need to ask about Pluto. It was nothing like Venus. With the fog, the stench, and the bugs, who would want to live on such a wretched planet? (If it even was a planet.)

"You are wavering between compassion and fear, between happiness and despair," Puck said, looking at me intently. "Are you from the planet earth?"

"I am. Are there other earth people here?"

"No. I haven't met any."

"Then how do you know about earth?" I asked.

"We knew about all of the planets on Venus. At night, we gazed at the skies admiring all of our brothers and sisters in the universe," Puck replied with a clouded expression on his lion face.

"I'd like to go home." I said, staring at Puck. "I wanted to return to Venus to learn how to cure my sick brother, but I've made a terrible mistake."

Water collected in the bottom corners of Puck's slit-shaped eyes. "This planet—or dwarf planet as some call it— is ruled by fear and every possible emotion that originates in fear. Pluto exists in a higher dimension than earth but negative. Every creature is self-serving and terrified of everyone else on Pluto."

I glanced over at Portia. What was she thinking? She lowered her head and pulled her wings in closer to her chest. Her thick lion's mane covered her eyes. She didn't utter a sound, but her lizard tail stood straight up behind her balled up body.

"Can anyone help me fix the balloon and go back to earth?" I pleaded. My shoulders and neck felt cold. Shivering, I folded my arms and tried to remember a warm summer day at the shore.

Puck averted his eyes. I couldn't tell if he was hiding something or if he just felt guilty. He turned to me and let out a big puff of air, "Pluto is like a black hole. Nothing ever escapes Pluto."

"What? I'm stuck here? I have to get home. My parents will be worried sick about me."

Now what? I should have trusted my instincts. I felt a pang of uneasiness when the balloon man didn't answer to the name Fagan, but I wasn't sure why at the time. Now I knew. This had to be a nightmare. It just had to be. I would wake up any second. *Wake up! Wake up!*

I slowly opened my eyes, expecting to see light from the hall bathroom streaming under my bedroom door. No, instead, I saw Puck bouncing on his hind legs with a softened glow in his glistening cat eyes. He was gently shaking his head back and forth.

"Help me fix my balloon. I'm desperate." I still couldn't cry. Believe me, I would have turned on the tears if I could have, but they were buried deep inside me. I stared intently at Puck and then Portia, hoping that my begging eyes would guilt them into helping me. No such luck. They weren't buying the guilt routine.

"How can we help you when we can't even help ourselves? We are trapped on this frozen half-planet with no way of getting home to Venus."

The word "trapped" kept blinking in my mind. I couldn't feel the cold anymore. My face grew hot and I began scratching my burning itchy skin, picking at the huge welts dotted across my arms. Portia stepped closer to me and patted her right wing on my back in a circling motion.

Puck must have read my mind, "My sister hasn't spoken since our imprisonment on Pluto. Terror seized her vocal chords. Even her thoughts are difficult to decipher."

"Does anyone else speak?"

"Plutonians never communicated with each other. They lived in fear, suspicious of the words and thoughts of others, afraid to utter a sound." Puck paused, softening his gaze. "But lately, something has changed. More and more beings release their thoughts out loud. It may be my imagination but I don't think so."

"Did you speak on Venus?" I asked.

"Usually, we communicated by thought. Sometimes we spoke just for the sheer joy of hearing each other's harmonic voices. You would call it singing. But here, on Pluto, it's different. It's hard to read the thoughts of others."

"You can read my mind, can't you?"

"Since you're from earth, you don't have the same energy as the Plutonians. Most of the beings on Pluto originate elsewhere in the solar system. I suspect others will understand you but they may not trust you."

"What language do they speak to each other?" I asked.

"Having separate languages is quite three dimensional. Even in a negative place like Pluto, the idea of separate languages is ludicrous."

"And your sister, will she ever communicate again?" I asked.

"Only if we go back home," Puck replied, lifting his gaze to the green murky sky.

"Why can't you go back home?"

"We became enslaved on Pluto eons ago. Danko, the head of Pluto, uses metallic alchemy to control us and all of the Plutonians." Puck shook his head and choked back a few tears. Portia couldn't look me in the eye, but I could hear her sniffling.

"How did Danko trap you on Pluto?" I asked, recognizing my own fate might not be any better than theirs.

"Ages and ages ago, we lived happily on Venus. Venusians knew that everything was alive, even the rocks and minerals. We could hear the subtle vibrations in the rocks and connect with them to create beautiful harmonies. All Venusians lived in harmony, whether they had two legs, a hundred legs, or just a tail. We were not afraid of each other and we respected our differences. But then something changed." Puck's voice trailed off. "The changes were so subtle at first; we hardly noticed the dark forces."

Puck dropped his head and let out a deep sigh. I glanced at Portia but she was still staring at her feet, tears pooling on the ground. I waited patiently for Puck to speak.

"A Dark Energy force named Danko arrived on Venus. He wanted to rule the entire universe," Puck said, cocking his head to the right and peeking at his chopped wing. "Venus was preparing to spiral up to another level of awareness and Danko couldn't let Venus slip away from him. He had to control us."

"How did he trick you?" I asked.

"Danko visited Venus and said he would teach us to fly if we would let him live among us. Before Danko spoke to us, we had never thought about flying. Venusians had always been happy as creeping, crawling creatures of the soil and water. But when Danko began to tempt us with thoughts of flying to the heavens, we simply couldn't resist. We agreed of our own free will to go to the mountains with Danko so he could teach us to fly."

"With those wings?" I questioned, pointing to Portia's back.

"No. These pathetic wings wouldn't lift a horsefly. I'm getting to that part." Puck hung his head low in shame.

"Danko instructed us to drink special chemicals that would make us grow wings. At first, we were delighted as our wings began to take shape. What we didn't realize was that the special wing-growing chemical was toxic to us. Of course, Danko knew that—he planned it that way. The chemicals reacted with the uranium inside of us. Uranium is the basic element of Venus—it is found inside all Venusians as carbon is in earth beings. Danko turned our bodies against us, like cancer growing out of control. The toxic elements reacted with our internal uranium, forming chemical compounds that crippled our DNA. With suppressed DNA, we no longer felt connected to each other and the rocks, lakes, and mountains. In our weakened minds, we were separate from every other creature. So, of course, we were frightened—terrified actually. Eventually, the Venusians who fell for Danko's tricks couldn't live on Venus. Our limited bodies with weak DNA were not compatible with the energy fields of Venus. Even the slightest movement pained us, as if we wore a coat of rocks. Portia and I feared transforming into living corpses—minds trapped in frozen bodies. Longing for one more burst of fun, we journeyed to a favorite amusement park near the sunflower fields. Although our cement bodies burned with pain, we looked forward to flying free on an amusement park ride one last time."

"I know that amusement park. That's where my balloon landed," I said.

Puck turned up his lips in a half-smile. He continued, "Portia spotted a roller coaster with a rickety wooden sign spelling out the name "Space Shifter" in lime green block letters. We had never seen it before. Curious about the new ride, my sister and I pressed our cement bodies into the last car and fastened the strange seaweed-colored seat belts. The roller coaster chugged along in a circular track, slowly at first. Our pain vanished as the roller coaster picked up speed. Faster and faster we twisted, climbing higher and higher. But, and this is the part I can barely admit to myself, we never returned to the starting point. We never saw any other Venusians on the ride. Instead, we exited the ride and found ourselves disembarking on Pluto. Right over there." Puck pointed to the dilapidated roller coaster. "We didn't realize it at first. But slowly the truth revealed itself—Danko had trapped us."

Puck drew in a deep breath, exhaled slowly, never looking up at me. I let the silence grow between us. Everything made sense and nothing made sense. I wondered if Pluto was where all of the missing Venusians went during the Great Transition. The horses at the carousel might be Asea's friends. Celeste's family members could be here somewhere, too. I could feel my chest muscles tighten as I began to question my own fate. How would I escape this horrid place?

"Why would Danko want to trap you?" I questioned.

"He says he is the supreme ruler," Puck replied. "He will not stop until he controls every corner of the universe."

I stared at Puck.

"I know what you're thinking," he said.

"What?"

"You're thinking how stupid we were for listening to Danko. Some of our horse friends were smarter than us. They didn't drink the toxic potion. They didn't care about flying to the heavens."

"I'm not judging you," I said. "I just want to get out of here." I still couldn't believe that I would be stuck on Pluto for all eternity. "Maybe you can design a rocket ship or airplane or hot air balloon or something," I suggested.

"No vehicle can transport us off Pluto. Even your balloon will not operate here," Puck explained, shaking his head back and forth. "See how it crashed."

"I thought it crashed because it wasn't mended right."

"Even if it were brand new, the balloon would not lift you off Pluto," Puck said, staring at the thickened sky.

"So you'll never go back home?"

"Our fears cripple us. We can't return to Venus until the chemicals in our blood are transmuted. We would die on Venus with so much toxic uranium coursing through our bodies."

"Could you escape Pluto and go to another planet?" I questioned.

"We want to go home just like you."

The three of us remained silent for a moment. I thought about the twins and their sad journey to enslavement on Pluto. I couldn't help but pity them. "Will you ever be able to break down Danko's chemical compounds?" I asked. "After a certain amount of time, the uranium might not be toxic anymore."

"No. It's not a question of time. Time is not the same here." Puck's face hardened. I thought he would morph into a statue again, but he didn't. "Pluto is like a black hole. Nothing escapes. Nothing. There's a big spiral of negative energy twisting around this place."

I chomped on his words, my mind buzzing. "There must be something."

"If we could find an element that could

reactivate our DNA, maybe we could return to Venus. Until then, we are imprisoned, frightened, and under the emotional control of Danko. The radiation in the uranium traps fear in our bodies. It's a vicious cycle. Each time we look at these pathetic deformed wings, we are reminded of our grave error and we spiral down a little further."

"Could you trick Danko into releasing you?"

"No. He's too calculating for that. We're stuck until we find a neutralizing element or mineral or until we find…" Puck stopped short.

"Until you find what? What else would help us get out of here?" I blurted out.

"There are rumors on Pluto, whisperings of something."

"Rumors of what?" I jumped up to within six inches of Puck's face. "What? Tell me."

"I shouldn't have said anything. I don't know what I was thinking."

"Tell me. Please," I begged.

"I don't know if the rumors are true. You can't trust Plutonians. Everyone is so afraid," Puck said, hanging his head low, his mane swishing back and forth, "but some speak of the secret notes."

"Secret notes?" I swallowed hard. Could they be the same secret notes the snake spoke of? "Where are they?"

"Generations of Plutonians have searched for the notes in Danko's castle, but no one has ever found them. If someone had, we'd all be free."

"Do you know anything else about them?" I asked, remembering the riddles from Venus.

Puck nodded, "I heard a riddle,

**Despite toxic stew, chemical storm,
The secret notes are in pure form".**

Puck whispered in my ear, never taking his eyes off his sister. "Searching through the castle will be treacherous because Danko wants the crystal in your pocket."

I knew Portia didn't want Puck telling me anything. The fur on her mane stood straight up and her mouth dropped wide open.

"My crystal?" I blurted out. As the words tumbled out of my mouth, I could feel a cold surge of energy slide down my backbone. He wanted my crystal just like the cop wanted Bradley's or rather my brother's. What for?

"Shhhh!" Puck appeared almost mad. The lines on his forehead deepened and his teeth jutted out. "Don't let Danko and his army of dimwits hear you. He'll kill us if we get in his way. One of his cohorts followed you in the field."

I shuddered remembering the footsteps in the shadows. I thought it was my imagination, my paranoia taking hold of me as I scurried through the swamp. But no—Danko had ordered his troops to stalk me.

In a barely audible voice, I repeated my question, "Why would he want my crystal?" My fingers remained wrapped tightly around the Aphrodite quartz.

"The crystal has power you can't imagine. On Venus, our elders sang about the brilliance of Venusian crystals. Danko knows of your crystal's capabilities." Puck's voice was getting louder. Portia looked over and motioned to Puck that he should be quiet.

"How am I going to find the secret notes? And even if I did, how will we escape Pluto?"

"The notes must include explicit directions on breaking through this dimension. If I knew what the secret notes said, I wouldn't need to find them. I'd have left Pluto ages ago." Puck shook his head back and forth. "Your crystal may guide you to the notes."

"I suppose I have no choice but to search the castle for the notes. My smashed balloon won't get me home," I said, trying to sound convincing, but I couldn't fool myself. I was terrified and would have done anything to be home with Michael and my parents.

"Be careful. Keep that crystal safely tucked away. If Danko knew I was talking to you he'd smash Portia and me into a thousand bits of crushed stone." The blaze in Puck's cat eyes proved he was serious.

"Where's—" The words were stuck in my

voicebox. I couldn't thrust out any words above a whisper. I cleared my throat and swallowed hard. "Where's his castle?"

"Over this bridge. A second inner moat rings around the perimeter of the castle. The castle's design includes circles within circles."

"Like a target," I murmured under my breath, feeling vulnerable. "Can you two come with me?"

"No, I'm sure we're being watched. At least seven lookout towers surround the outer walls of his castle." Puck tried to reassure me adding, "We'll meet you inside later. You have to go now. Danko's guardsmen probably know I'm talking to you. Good-bye."

Puck and Portia hopped back onto their marble pedestals at the foot of the bridge and, in a poof, turned back to stone. I wanted to turn around and race back through the field to the hot air balloon. But what for? A demolished balloon? I pinched the skin below my thumb. *Wake up! Wake up!* But the nightmare rolled on. I didn't want to go into the castle. I'd have done almost anything to avoid it, but I had no options. The hard landing destroyed the balloon—I couldn't fix it. If I lingered outside the castle, someone or something would capture me. I'd be a deer in an open field waiting for a hunter to shoot. I thought of my mother. In times of crisis, she would never sit back and just accept her fate. She would do something—anything—to improve the situation. I had no choice. I would just have to slip into the castle and find the secret notes. That's all I could do.

CHAPTER 10
A Risky Decision

Clenching my teeth, I tiptoed onto the bridge, but then I turned back like a kid afraid to jump off the high diving board. My stomach ached, my head throbbed and my legs weighed a hundred pounds each. Although I tried, I couldn't push my feet across the bridge. Fear glued them in place.

Sliding my right hand into my pocket, I stroked the Aphrodite quartz. I struggled to remember Venus, but the image flickered on and off in my mind. Turning back one more time, I thought I saw Portia wink at me with her violet-red eyes. I forced a smile and winked back at her marble body before stepping onto the stone bridge.

The trek across the bridge did not take nearly long enough. Shortly, a round stone castle colored a hideous smoke-streaked gray emerged from behind the thinning green fog. I counted at least twenty-two windows facing me, but they appeared boarded up. Jagged iron shutters crossed in front of each window. I could see three lookout towers jutting out from the enormous structure. If I could see the towers, then someone in the towers could see me. Someone could be watching me, studying me, waiting for me. A cold wave of fear sucked the air out of my lungs, leaving my skin itching with welts.

Snap! Snap!

What was that? I peered under the bridge and saw crocodiles munching on fuzzy, blood-red creatures. Fluorescent green fish with fangs swam in circles around the crocodiles, hungry for dinner. The putrid smell of rotting flesh hung in the air. Was I next? Would the crocodiles mount the bridge and devour me alive?

I stopped for a moment, thinking I could turn back and run away. Of course, I couldn't. Where would I go? The only thing I had, the only thing that gave me any comfort, was my Aphrodite quartz tucked in my jean pocket. I continued on, scratching the welts that blanketed my arms and chest until blood seeped through my shirt. After reaching the opposite end of the bridge, I crouched down on a patch of swampy ground separating the outer moat from a second moat. Without warning, the wooden drawbridge dropped into horizontal position over the inner moat. Danko's troops had come to capture me or maybe Danko himself! My heart thumped wildly in my chest as I tucked my body into a tight ball and waited behind an iron post, never taking my eyes off the drawbridge. What or who planned to attack me? Where could I go? I waited and waited. Nothing happened. I waited a bit longer, my head growing heavy with drowsiness.

Crackling twigs and swishing leaves jolted me awake. Sensing eyes glaring at the back of my neck, I twitched my shoulders and tried to shake off the stalker feeling. I knew I couldn't just stay there and surrender. I had to escape.

Crawling on my hands and knees I crept for what seemed like hours through the ten-foot wide patch of grass encircling the inner moat. My bloody knees and palms burned but I kept moving forward, feeling certain someone watched me. When I couldn't crawl one more inch, I stopped suddenly and the air became eerily silent. Maybe the sound of rustling leaves had come from a harmless animal I tried to convince myself.

I noted that the castle looked exactly the same from every angle. It was a perfect circle with boarded up windows and seven symmetrical black watchtowers perched atop the castle roof. From the watchtowers, the guardsmen could see the amusement park, the bridge, my broken balloon. It was painfully obvious I had nowhere to hide.

Again, the crunching of twigs and leaves startled me. I stopped crawling and as soon as I did I could feel eyes lasering the back of my neck. My limbs cramped up in fear.

"You're hard to keep up with," a husky female voice whispered.

I couldn't move my arms or legs. I couldn't speak either. Game over.

"Fear not," the faceless voice rasped.

I wanted to appear brave, to cry out

something threatening, but I couldn't make my body cooperate. *Breathe. Breathe.* It was all I could do to muster the strength to lift my right hand off the ground and place it in my pocket. The crystal remained safely hidden. Slowly, I released the air in my lungs trying to remain positive but knowing I had little hope. I dared not turn around and face my stalker until I knew her motivation.

"Why are you following me?" I squeaked.

"You know why."

I whipped my head around to see the speaker. No one was there.

"I'm on the ground," the voice said, but now it sounded like two or three voices.

I knew those voices. How could I forget? The three-headed snake was back. I searched the dirt for her. Nothing but dried up underbrush. Keeping my eyes focused on the ground, I noticed a creature slithering near my left knee.

"How did you get here?" I asked, still unable to move.

"I'm a hologram. I project my image out into the cosmos at will. I can solidify if need be."

"But why?"

"How many times do I have to repeat myself?" she grumbled. "I must have the secret notes. I am growing tired of your childish games."

"If you are a hologram as you say, you don't need me to escape Pluto. What do you need the secret notes for?" I asked.

"Danko has controlled them long enough. His reign of horror is over—that is if you'll help me."

"Why don't you find them yourself?"

"Regretfully, I need an earth being."

"How about a Venusian? Or a Plutonian?" I suggested.

"Earth is the next planet scheduled to jump to the fourth dimension unless Danko gets his way. The secret notes must be located by an earth being."

"But I thought you said the notes were on earth."

"I was wrong. They're in that castle because Danko wouldn't let them get too far away from him."

"So you know Danko well?"

"Unfortunately, I do. I convinced him to fight his brother in a duel a long time ago." The snake let the hoods over her eyes drop. "I can't believe I'm talking about it. I never discuss my past, but you ought to know what you're up against. "

"Why would you want Danko to fight his brother?" I questioned. "Why would you care?"

"Revenge. Danko destroyed my family with his nuclear experiments."

"So you wanted his brother to destroy him?" I asked.

"I thought I could fix the fight. I had it all figured out. I inserted a crystal in Danko's brother's shield, thinking he would humiliate Danko, but

Danko won the duel because he switched the shields." The snake twisted her heads slowly and stared at me. "That was the beginning of the end of my beloved planet."

"What planet?"

"Maldek. It's nothing but chunks of rock now," the snake said, her twisted heads swaying back and forth. "You know Maldek as the asteroid belt between Mars and Jupiter."

"What happened to Maldek?"

"Nuclear war! Danko convinced half the planet to attack his brother's half."

"Why?"

"He wanted control of Maldek, but in the end no one had control, neither him nor his brother. Maldek blew up in a horrific nuclear war. But that's not your concern now. You need to find the secret notes."

"I don't know if I can find them."

"Don't you want to cure your brother?" she reminded me.

"I made things worse at home with the crystal and now my brother is back in the hospital." I lifted my palms off the ground and wiped my eyes with the back of my hand. "It's all a mistake," I insisted.

"It's no mistake. Danko lured you here. When he saw the crop circle in your backyard, he knew you had the crystal."

"How did he lure me? I wanted to go to

Venus on the hot air balloon but wound up here by accident."

The snake twisted all three heads at once. "It was no accident. Nothing in this universe is an accident."

"How did Danko make the balloon land here?"

"Remember the Labor Day Carnival?"

"Yes."

"Remember the freaky ride attendant at the Haunted Maze?"

"Yes."

"That was Danko," the snake said, lifting the hoods off all six eyes.

"Danko?"

"He frightened you."

"I know."

"The balloon latched onto your thoughts and landed here."

"You can't be serious," I piped up.

"I'm dead serious," she said spinning her three heads and sausage body around and around. "You're stuck here without the secret notes. Go find them."

I gulped hard. "You think they're in the castle?"

"I do."

"How do I sneak into the castle?"

"I never thought you'd ask." The snake

145

tightened her three smiles and blew out a puff of air before speaking. "Circle back to the drawbridge and wait by the iron post. I'll bite the guardsman in the lookout tower. He'll be distracted, writhing in pain. You can walk across the drawbridge when you hear the ear-piercing screech."

"I thought you were only a hologram."

"Solid matter is nothing but energy vibrating very slowly, painfully slow." She moved closer to me. I thought I felt her breath on the back of my leg.

"I believe you. You don't have to bite me."

"I'll see you inside." The snake slinked away not nearly as threatening as before. Still I wondered if I could trust her.

I crawled around to the front of the castle with my palms and knees numb from the friction. Within a short while, a long shrill yelp punctured the silence. That was my cue to enter the castle. I stood up but hesitated, gripped by a growing fear. My knees buckled and my head swayed back and forth. I grabbed the railing and pressed my legs forward a few inches, but my feet wore cement block shoes. Should I step onto the drawbridge? Or should I run back to the twins and hide in the marsh? I had only a moment to decide. Someone would be watching from the tower shortly. I had to make my move.

I tapped the edge of the drawbridge with my left foot, keeping weight on my right. I could run at any moment. But where? I had no balloon. I had nowhere to hide. I might as well go in the castle and search for the notes. A moving target is harder to strike.

With caution, I began my trek across the bridge. After taking three or four steps, I detected rumbling movement under my feet. Someone lifted the drawbridge! I reached out for the railing, but my sweaty palms slipped. As the drawbridge moved upward, I slid down. Again, I reached out to squeeze the side railing. Somehow, I grabbed a piece of it, but now I dangled over the water—directly above the crocodiles and flesh-eating fish! Clutching the railing, I pulled my limp body back onto the drawbridge seconds before it snapped into closed position. With a thump an iron gate slammed down vertically, trapping me in the entrance.

Immediately, a sharp clanking sound filled the air. I cupped my hands over my ears, but that made little difference. I couldn't think clearly with the high-pitched noise. Plus, I couldn't see anything. I slipped my right hand into my pocket and stroked the crystal, energized by the warmth. What kind of place was this? I couldn't see my fingers two inches in front of my face.

Blindly, I took a step forward, but there was no solid ground. Dropping at least ten feet into a pit, I landed on my left side, my head smacking against the concrete floor. I yelped out as intense pain rippled through my body, but no one heard me. Maybe that was a good thing. I'm not sure I wanted anyone to hear me.

I might have blacked out and laid there for a period of time. When my head stopped spinning, I took stock of my options. To the best of my knowledge, I was imprisoned in a dungeon, with no escape plan, no allies, and not a hint of where I was. My mind flashed back to the cunning snake. She might have lured me onto the bridge so that Danko could steal my crystal. I was just a prop in her well-devised plan. But that didn't make sense because she gave me the crystal on Venus. If she wanted Danko to have it, she would have offered it to him not me. Nothing made any sense.

I closed my eyes and promptly the ear-splitting sound stopped. In the blackness, I felt small and alone. I attempted to stand up, but my legs had become so feeble, I sank to my kneecaps. Again, I struggled to stand. With one knee pressed against the concrete floor, I inhaled deeply and slowly pulled myself up to a standing position. A ray of light streamed down from a crack in the ceiling, like a flashlight beam. Total darkness engulfed me except for the cone of light radiating through the ceiling crevice. I could now make out a door to the left and one to the right.

I chose the door to the right. I wrapped my blistered hand around the knob and turned it slowly. Holding my breath, I gently pushed open the door.

Absolute silence. Thoughts of doom screamed in my head. Were Danko's troops preparing to ambush me? I could see no one.

Faint cones of light seeped through baseball-sized cuts in the ceiling at least six feet over my head. I waited for my pupils to adapt to the weak lighting before stepping through the doorway. I couldn't help but wonder if that was the "light" concealing the secret notes that Asea had mentioned. No, the hiding place couldn't be that simple. Could it be?

I walked a few steps. After bumping into a stone wall, I knew the corridor was circular, not straight. I patted down the walls, searching for a doorknob. Nothing, just stone. I started to doubt my decision to take the door on the right, but it was too late to turn back. I walked a few more steps. The pressure in my shins and knees suggested the floor sloped downward. I was descending deeper and deeper below ground, spiraling into a lower basement. Or was it a tomb? A dank odor filled the space around me and the hot metal taste grew stronger almost cooking my taste buds.

I pressed on. My eyes were working better now. The sound of my sneakers rubbing against the concrete echoed through the hallway. With no other noise to distract me, I couldn't turn down the volume of my thoughts. I felt so alone—like a kid lost at an amusement park except my parents wouldn't be waiting for me at the information booth. I had gotten myself into a terrible mess and I was the only one who could save me. I didn't have Michael.

Straight ahead I could just make out a shiny metallic ball, which I took to be a doorknob, jutting into the corridor. I stopped in front of the door and analyzed the wood carvings inscribed near the top. Tilting my chin toward the ceiling, I could make out the word "Aries" carved in capital letters each about the length of my hand. Etched in the wood directly below "ARIES" was a ram standing proudly. My eyes lingered on the ram until they grew too weak from straining. I could feel exhaustion pressing my shoulders down, but I couldn't just collapse and give up.

Someone was coming.

CHAPTER 11
The Confrontation

The sound of echoing footsteps scissored through me, causing my leg muscles to tighten. My heart began beating rapidly against my rib cage and I could feel my throat closing up. I stood still, perking my ears to locate the source of the noise. The shuffles came from behind me. I turned the doorknob. *Please open.* It was locked. I pushed it, jiggled it, and twisted it repeatedly. The knob didn't budge. With the thud of each footstep louder than the one before, the stalker was closing the gap. I could sense the stare of cold eyes penetrating my skin, studying my every move, but I didn't dare turn around. Again, I fumbled with the brass knob, praying the door would open. No. The door was locked. I tried to run hoping adrenaline would thrust my legs forward, but my legs betrayed me and I froze.

A thunderous voice boomed through the corridor. I knew without looking that Danko stood behind me. I cowered like a little kid called down to the principal's office, certain he knew how frightened I was.

"Who gave you permission to enter my castle?"

Words clumped up in my throat. Only a low croaking sound came out, "I-I—I—"

"You are trespassing. Turn around and show me some respect," Danko growled.

I couldn't face him. My heart beat so fast it seemed to stop cold. Hot tears scorched my eyeballs, but I kept the water flow dammed up. Danko would not see me cry.

"Have you come to give me your crystal?"

"No," I squeaked out.

"I want your Aphrodite quartz crystal. Give it to me."

I inched my right hand into my jean pocket and clasped the crystal between my index finger and thumb. The crystal radiated a subtle warmth, reassuring me, if only for a passing moment. Or maybe it was just the heat from my thigh that warmed the crystal. Whatever the reason, I felt a little better knowing I had the crystal with me. I closed my eyes and tried to shore up the strength to confront Danko.

Clearing the lump out of my throat, with my back still facing him, I asked, "What do you want with it?"

"That crystal guarantees the survival of planet Pluto—and for the record Pluto is a planet. My planet."

"What survival?"

"Look, Boy! I don't like your questions. Give me the crystal or you will perish on Pluto."

"I'm not going to hand over the crystal

without knowing why you want it." I hoped I sounded brave, but I knew better. I knew he'd strike me from the venom in his voice.

Danko inched closer. I could feel his steamy breath on the back of my neck creeping down my spine. It was that same dragon breath I smelled at the Haunted Maze. Was he about to pounce for the crystal? My muscles tensed up in anticipation of pain, like I was getting a shot. I kept my trembling fingers wrapped tightly around the Aphrodite quartz. He'd have to pry my fist open with a razor-sharp knife to steal the crystal. No way was he getting it now. I had come too far.

I held my breath. Icicle nails tapped my left shoulder, numbing the nerves, and making me think I should just hand over the crystal. *Wake up! Wake up!* This had to be a nightmare! The frozen fingers clutched my shoulder, whipping my neck around 180 degrees. I had come face to face with a monster.

Before me stood a grotesque creature, more dead than a corpse. Dime-sized pits dotted his decaying face with a light-colored fluid oozing out of the holes. The dim lighting saved me from getting a really good look at him, but I could see his eyes. His piercing yellow goopy eyes glared at me, causing my stomach to ball up in a fist. I couldn't look at his face but somehow it was familiar. Not the ride attendant— someone else. Where had I seen him before? I knew this evil face. I stared at my feet and then lifted my eyes just long enough to capture a quick glance. He was the policeman who came to my door with Mr. Jenkins! He was Danson—the bully who had manipulated Bradley into handing over the crystal which was really Michael's crystal. I hung my head low so he couldn't see my fear.

"Look at me, you defiant little crumb." Danko snarled.

I lifted my eyes slightly, but kept my head down and my mouth shut.

"If I control your crystal, I control earth. Understand?"

I needed to stall for more time. "You don't control earth from Pluto. No one does." I kept my head hung low, wondering if it was the crystal giving me the strength to be so brazen.

"You think so? You had better rethink the junk science they teach you in school." Danko placed his bony decomposing hand under my chin and jerked my head so I had to look at him. I felt woozy but somehow remained standing.

"Why do you want to control earth? We're billions of miles away from you," I whispered.

"Earth is the last third dimensional planet in this solar system. All the other planets have jumped to higher dimensions."

"Like Venus."

"Before Venus jumped to the fourth dimension, I tempted a few sorry creatures into coming with me, like those twin blocks of plaster you met outside," Danko cackled. "They thought they could fly. Dimwits!"

I swallowed hard thinking of Puck and Portia. I couldn't let Danko know how frightened I was. "So what if earth is the last third dimensional planet? What does that matter?" I asked, thinking I sounded tough.

"I need control because I don't want earth spiraling up. Life on earth is full of pain, fear, and isolation. You know that. You tried to drown your brother," Danko snickered.

"I did not! I love him!"

"The fear that strangles earth, that tortures you, is the lifeblood of Pluto. I cannot have you earth beings replacing fear with love and compassion. I need war, hatred, and complete paranoia!"

"But —how does our fear help you?"

"It's all about balance in this solar system. If earth jumps to a higher dimension, Pluto will get sucked into a black hole, reduced to a pinpoint. And then where would I, the master of Pluto, be?" The fire in his eyes made my heart drop to my stomach. "The solar system would not tolerate the negative energy of Pluto if earth were positively aligned. I will not be diminished to a speck of dust."

I still didn't understand the connection between the Aphrodite quartz and Earth or Pluto for that matter. I imagined it had something to do with

155

the mind of the crystal. Somehow the crystal was conscious and able to connect with other seemingly inanimate objects like the planet Earth. Even if I didn't know how the crystal tapped into the earth's mind, I would have to trust that it had some kind of magic.

Clenching the crystal between my fingers, I kept my hand in my pocket, my eyes locked on Danko. I let the silence grow between us, but did not blink. I was holding my ground, teetering between hope and despair.

His flickering eyes spun around in their sockets. "I need total control. Right now, earth is perfectly balanced between love and fear. It could go either way, but I can't take a risk." With each word, his voice boomed louder, crashing through my eardrums. "I demand your Aphrodite quartz," Danko growled.

"What are you going to do with the crystal?" I twirled it in my pocket, my hand shaking.

"Your Aphrodite quartz fits into mine like a puzzle to form a double tetrahedron. They're twin crystals."

"Where did you get your crystal?" I asked playing dumb.

"From a dopey kid at the carnival," Danko replied. "He's almost as stupid as you. If you hadn't buried your Aphrodite quartz in the field, I never would have seen the crop circle. I never would have known how to get my hands on Venusian twin crystals."

"You're not getting my crystal," I insisted, thinking back to the Haunted Maze. Danko looked different from the creepy carnival guy but the energy was the same.

"I don't know why you didn't just give me the crystal at the Haunted Maze," Danko said out of nowhere.

"Haunted Maze? How did you know about that?" I bluffed.

"I am the master of Pluto. You should have given me the crystal and saved yourself a whole lot of trouble," Danko scoffed.

"What are you talking about?"

"With the twin Venusian crystals, I control the spin of the giant solid iron core crystal at the center of the earth. When the north and south poles switch places, as they have before, I will dominate earth!" Danko's head was shaking as he pounded his fists in the air.

"An iron crystal at the center of the earth?"

"Yes," Danko smirked.

"How do you know that? No one has ever visited the earth's core."

"You're such a fool! We know everything about earth, from the surface to the core," Danko said smugly. "Our energy vibrates at a faster rate so you can't see us but we can see you. Too bad! Give me that crystal!"

"I need it to help my brother." I said without thinking.

"You're going to help your brother, are you?" Danko mocked. "We'll see about that."

"I will never give you the crystal."

"You are no match for me, the master of Pluto. When I get that crystal, and I will get it, I'll spin the earth's iron core so that the iron in your human blood goes cold."

Danko's desperate shrieks forced me to believe him. He was not going to stop until he controlled the earth and I, foolishly, stood in his way. Vomit rose up in my throat, but I swallowed it back down. My right hand was still tucked in my jean pocket, my fingers wrapped tightly around the crystal. I dug my nails into my flesh. *Wake up! Wake up!* Suddenly, Danko lunged at me, grabbing my shirt three inches below my throat and shaking me violently. "Give it to me!" he shrieked.

I struggled to deflect his attack with my left hand, but I wasn't too coordinated being right-handed. Danko threw his weight on me and I collapsed to the floor. His hot breath brought the vomit back up and I pushed it back down. Then, with my left hand, I stretched out my fingers and clawed at Danko's right eye. A big chunk of his eyeball got stuck under my nails—his eye crumbling like a hard-boiled egg. Only a few jagged chunks remained in the socket. Danko drew his two hands to his eye socket and howled in anguish.

"You and I are not finished," he warned. "You will pay for what you have done to me and you will pay dearly. We'll see how much you love your brother." Then, abruptly, in a dusty cloud of chemicals, Danko vanished as quickly as he appeared. Was it a trick? A hologram? I was too frightened to think clearly. I had to get away.

I sprinted down the circular corridor trying to erase the image of Danko. The skin covering my neck and shoulder blades itched again. The itch spread, rippling down my arms and back. I wanted to scratch my skin until I bled, but I couldn't. Instead, I ran harder. But there was nowhere to go. The metallic taste, stronger than before, stuck to my tongue. I gathered spit in my mouth and swallowed, but the taste lingered. Where could I run? I needed to find the secret notes and get out of there.

My eyes focused straight ahead, the glimmer of a shiny doorknob at least twenty feet ahead beckoned me. I didn't think I could run any further, but I kept moving. The frigid, coppery air burned my chest, forming a lump of acid in my throat. Stopping for a moment in front of the door, I inhaled as deeply as I could, but little air made the trip to my lungs. The word "LEO" was inscribed near the top of the door, just as "ARIES" had been etched in the first door. My eyes focused on the carving of a majestic lion under the letters. Was there a door for every zodiac sign?

I cupped my ear against the door, but heard nothing. I tried the knob. It was locked. Should I knock on the door? What if one of Danko's guards grabbed me? I kept moving.

I hadn't taken ten steps when I found myself before a door with the word 'SAGITTARIUS' inscribed in the wood. Just below it, a beautiful carving of a mythological figure, half man and half horse, caught my eye. The faint sound of distant moaning rumbled from behind the door. The muffled sound was so slight that I wouldn't have heard it if I hadn't pressed my ear against the door. Were Puck and Portia calling for me? They said they would meet me inside. Maybe something happened to them.

I clutched the brass knob and was surprised when it turned. That could be a good thing or a bad thing. I cracked the door open about a foot and peered inside. The room appeared to be a dark closet. I stepped into the room, straining my eyes to see. The space reminded me of the cellar in my grandma's house with stale underground air mixed with paint thinner and sulfur. I couldn't identify the smell exactly, but it tasted poisonous, and every cell in my body screamed in protest.

The moaning was louder now and not one voice but a chorus of wailing voices. I didn't have time to figure out the source of the screams because with a loud swoosh, the door slammed behind me. I spun around to open the door, but I couldn't find the knob. My hands moved up and down the door, pressing against the wood, but the door wouldn't budge. I was locked in a black void.

CHAPTER 12
The Stone Labyrinth

A single tear dripped out of the corner of my left eye. Instinctively, I delved into my pocket and pulled out the Aphrodite quartz. Not only did the crystal radiate the purple grid of light I had grown to depend on, but now a curious hot energy, more intense than usual, nearly burned my fingers. It was as if my thoughts switched the crystal into active mode.

Clasping the crystal between my thumb and index finger, I searched for the doorknob. But I couldn't even find the door! I waved the crystal to the left and then to the right, straining to see my exact location. The room appeared like a cave with stone walls surrounding me, reaching well over my head. The walls did not touch the ceiling, falling short by at least a foot. I pushed against the walls with all my weight, but the stone didn't budge. As my eyes adjusted to the glow of the crystal, I noticed that the stone walls veered to the right. I held my arm out and paced along the twisting path, still gripping the crystal between my fingers.

"Jack, we're over here," a familiar male voice whispered.

"Puck?"

"Yes."

"How'd you know I was here?" I asked.

"I created a picture of your mind by connecting with your energy stream."

"I can't see you, Puck."

"We're about ten feet in front of you caught between the crevices of two stone walls."

"How did you get here?" I asked, wondering if Danko was tricking me.

"We slid into the moat, careful not to attract attention and swam to a trap door in the rear of the castle. After crawling through water pipes, we followed your energy to this cave. But now we're stuck."

"Stuck?"

"Our tails are trapped between the stone blocks in the walls."

"I only have the light from the Aphrodite quartz," I said. "I'll try to dislodge you."

I tugged gently on Puck's tail, sliding his tail up and down the crevice an inch or two. It would not budge. I stopped for a moment and tried to help Portia. She didn't speak but grunted as I attempted to release her. For what seemed like ten or fifteen minutes, I switched back and forth between the twins trying to free them. At one point, I thought I was close to freeing Portia's tail, but then it swelled up.

"Can you turn to marble and break free?" I asked.

"No, if we transform into statues, we'll crumble into a million pieces from the pressure. It's never wise to morph into stone unless your physical body is free," Puck said.

"Let me see what caused you to get stuck."

Using the crystal as a flashlight, I moved it slowly over Puck's lizard tail, looking for the source of the ensnarement. The more I pulled, the more snug his tail became, as if it were knotted in the wall.

"Does it hurt?" I asked.

"I can handle physical pain."

As I tugged at their tails, a peculiar burning odor seeped through the cave, stinging my nostrils and burning my throat. This was the kind of smell that makes you run for the nearest exit. I knew we had to leave the cave immediately, although I couldn't see any smoke.

"I know you are worried. You can leave us if you want to," Puck offered.

"I'm not going anywhere without you two," I insisted.

Then an amazing thing happened, something I never would have expected. Trying to loosen Portia's tail, I brushed my crystal against the stone wall. Abruptly, the wall retreated, shifting back at least a foot. Portia fell forward on her face and paws as she snapped her tail free. The corners of her mouth lifted to a half grin—the closest thing to a smile I had seen on her face.

"What happened?" Puck asked, his tail still locked in the crevice.

"The crystal moved the wall!"

I still couldn't believe it but I wasn't wasting time trying to figure it out. I touched the wall behind Puck with the Aphrodite quartz. As if on cue, the stone wall recoiled, releasing Puck's lizard tail.

"What kind of magic is in this crystal?" I asked.

"The crystal is alive or aware or something," Puck said. "Now you know why Danko wants it so badly."

"I can't give this crystal to Danko. Somehow I'm going to find the secret notes, get off this planet and cure my brother."

The three of us huddled together, trudging through the twisting path. "Do you think we're getting closer to an exit door?" Puck asked. "Maybe the path is a circle."

I didn't know whether to go left, right or turn back around. My eyes were stinging so badly I could scarcely keep them open—like someone sprayed bathroom cleaner in my face. My head was spinning. Whether the dizziness came from walking in circles, breathing the toxic air, or being exhausted, I couldn't be certain. All I knew was if I didn't find an exit soon, I'd suffocate.

At the next crossing point, we stepped to the left. My shoelace snagged the toothed edge of a rock and I stumbled forward. As I braced myself, the crystal slammed into the wall on my right, causing the wall to draw back immediately. I jumped in disbelief.

With the unexpected shift in the walls, the faint moaning sounds grew louder. Clasping the crystal, I pushed my hand in the new space between the two walls. I could hear chanting and screaming, but couldn't figure out the source of the anguished cries. The distinct odor of charred flesh or hair assaulted my nose. I knew I shouldn't look, but I had to—just like I have to look at car crashes on the side of the road. I clenched my teeth and held my breath as I peered behind the wall to see who was screaming.

The glow of a raging fire cast light on a spacious room, at least fifteen feet below me, about the size of a school gymnasium. A circle of bird-like figures with gray clumps on their backs looped around the central flame. Each creature was trapped in an individual copper cage, chained with its back to the roaring fire. The ceiling stretched at least thirty feet into the air but was not visible because billowing greenish-grey smoke blocked the view. With limited vision, I couldn't make out whether the flames touched the creatures, but something made them howl in pain. As my eyes adjusted to the firelight, I realized that the creatures had almost human faces, like fairies. Who were these fairies? Why did Danko cage them? The further I ventured into Danko's castle, the more questions I had.

"Can I see?" Puck asked.

I stepped back and he pressed his face in the area between the walls. "I've never seen this before. I've never even heard about this dungeon. To think we've been trapped on Pluto for ages and we've never heard the wailing fairies. Perhaps they drank a chemical potion to grow wings and became trapped on Pluto."

"Maybe," I mumbled.

And then it hit me. As Puck spoke, I realized who the fairies might be—Celeste's brothers and sisters! Celeste said they wanted to fly to earth. Maybe they drank the toxic potion on Venus hoping to grow wings and found themselves imprisoned on Pluto. I felt responsible for them, like I would be letting Celeste down if I didn't free them too.

I had ignored my burning chest and stinging eyes for as long as I could, but now I couldn't deny the toxic chemicals anymore. My lungs labored to suck in the tiniest amount of air. I imagined an airplane's oxygen mask plopping down from the ceiling and in my mind I breathed in pure oxygen. Struggling to hold a mental picture of the yellow mask, I blinked.

"We've got to find a way out of here. I don't think I can stay in the cave much longer."

Portia stroked my back with her wing and nodded. Then, the three of us silently marched ahead, with my crystal illuminating the path. Puck and

167

Portia remained two steps behind me, their wings overlapping. I wanted to be brave, but it was only a matter of time before my oxygen supply ran out. I would have to come back for Celeste's siblings once I had a rescue plan.

"We can't just keep walking. We're spiraling deeper and deeper into this maze with no way out," I warned.

"You called this a maze," Puck blurted out.

"What would you call it?"

"I thought this was the stone labyrinth of Plutonian folklore. Some remember a time when Plutonians strolled freely through the labyrinth. This must be it, right?" Puck asked.

"No. No. No. There are breaks in the path where we have to choose left or right. Labyrinths don't have decision points." I paused, not wanting to offend Puck. "This stone cave of twisting paths and trails is a maze."

"That makes no sense," Puck insisted.

I was losing patience. The pungent air made my head woozy and it was all I could do to stand straight and keep moving. We needed to escape the maze or we'd all die. Or at least I would. Maybe the Venugan twins could survive without oxygen, but I knew I couldn't.

"It can't be a labyrinth," I paused, choking back a few tears.

"So this is a stone maze?" Puck questioned.

"Where is the stone labyrinth if this isn't it?"

"Maybe if we find the legendary stone labyrinth we'll find the secret notes," I suggested.

"Maybe," Puck answered but he didn't sound convinced.

I marched forward, still puzzled by the maze. I had strolled through two labyrinths: the glass labyrinth under the amusement park on Venus and the one in Mr. Jenkin's cornfield. In both instances, I ended up in the same place I started, never having to make a choice at a break in the path. The Galactic Library stood at the center of the glass labyrinth but there were no forks in the road, no dead ends. This stone maze couldn't be a labyrinth.

Or could it?

A far-fetched idea exploded in my mind—like fireworks. What if the maze used to be a labyrinth? My heart quickened as a rush of adrenaline zipped through my veins. I jumped up on the balls of my feet, spun around, and looked at Puck and Portia.

"What is it?" Puck asked me. "You're so animated. Your thoughts are running wild."

I inhaled deeply, clutching my crystal tightly. "Maybe sections of the stone walls in the labyrinth were moved deliberately to confuse Plutonians. Now the labyrinth is a maze."

"Let me get this straight," Puck said slowly. "Danko destroyed the labyrinth because he couldn't allow the Plutonians to find the hidden dungeon. He was hiding the secret notes."

"If we move these walls back to a labyrinth form, we'll end up where we started in the zodiac corridor," I added. "And maybe we'll find the secret notes and get out of here."

Immediately, I began pressing the stone walls with the Aphrodite quartz. As if commanded by the crystal, vast sections of heavy rock retreated like soldiers, without making so much as a swoosh sound. My crystal appeared to tap into the mind of the stone, directing the stone walls. I wondered if the crystal could construct a building or a pyramid on earth. It was the coolest thing I had ever seen.

As each wall moved into position, subtle changes occurred in my immediate surroundings. Slowly, at first, slender light beams seeped into the cave, but strangely there were no windows or peep holes. Perhaps I imagined them. The acrid air that had seared my lungs did not burn quite as much or taste quite as poisonous. I could take deeper and deeper breaths and more oxygen was reaching my brain. As we restored the labyrinth, I felt more peaceful. We were making progress.

Soon the labyrinth stood in perfect order. It appeared that the circular labyrinth was sandwiched between the spiraling zodiac door corridor and the lower level dungeon where the fairies were caged. Danko's castle was circles within circles, just as Puck indicated. But where were the secret notes?

"This is fantastic," Puck said, tapping his sister with his left wing. Her eyes glimmered.

I thought Portia would say something, anything, but she remained silent, her lips partially covered by her mane.

"The notes must be here somewhere. Why else would Danko have destroyed the labyrinth?" I asked. "He had to be hiding something."

"Let's loop around and see what we uncover," Puck suggested.

I pinched my eyes shut and conjured up an image of the secret notes. I envisioned a large black snakeskin book something similar to a hard cover dictionary. Would the notes be concealed in a book like the books in the Galactic Library? Or maybe they were scrolls of papyrus paper tucked inside a box. It would be so much easier if we had seen them already, if we knew what we were looking for.

"It makes sense that they're here in the labyrinth," I mumbled, "but they're supposed to be in a box in the light."

"It's dark in here."

"I know. I'm just thinking out loud."

I was so distracted I didn't detect the piercing eyes watching me, stalking me and the twins.

CHAPTER 13
Into the Dungeon

"What are you doing?" a scratchy female voice demanded. The voice was deeper than the three-headed snake's, but honestly I wished it were only the snake. As least I knew what to expect from her. This voice spooked me.

I held my breath for a moment, too petrified to turn around and face my stalker. Hoping that Danko's crony didn't see my crystal, I quickly stuck the Aphrodite quartz into my front pocket. My fingers remained twisted around the crystal, forming a fist in my jean pocket.

"What did you stick in your pocket?" she asked.

My vocal chords twisted up. I tried to snap back a clever response, something that would make this grunt shut up and disappear, but my mind drew a blank.

"N-N-Nothing."

"You know it's something," she snipped.

"I-I-I'm not doing anything," I told her.

"You are destroying Danko's maze and now you're going to pay for your crime."

Bony cold fingers, lighter in touch than Danko's, tapped me on the left shoulder. "You'd better fix this maze or you'll be solid waste."

I shuddered, my feet frozen in place. I still couldn't turn around. The muted sound of Portia sniffling and sobbing echoed through the cave and I hoped the twins would break free even if I couldn't. Closing my eyes, I tried to imagine an escape route. I spun the crystal in my pocket and, capturing a burst of energy, sassed back. "I am fixing it. I'm restoring the form of the stone labyrinth." I turned and faced the intruder.

It was more female than male, with scaly skin tinged bluish grey. Her swollen eyes were deep red, the color of dried blood. She had no eyebrows but, in lieu of eyelashes, what looked like spider legs dangled from her forehead. Unruly clumps of steely grey hair swept the floor. Her fingers, capped by pointy crimson nails, stretched out from under the sleeves of a ragged silver gown. Wrapped around her scrawny neck was a necklace comprised of several strands of copper chain.

I gasped in horror, feeling a glob of acid burn my throat, but I could not let her sense my terror. Danko must have sent her to seize the crystal, and I wouldn't give it up without a fight. I locked eyes with her, trying not to blink, trying to disguise my utter despair.

"Danko trusted me, the mighty Nix, to straighten the maze and imprison the three of you."

"We haven't done anything wrong," I said, but my voice faltered.

"Correct the maze or I will chain you in a place so horrific, no being ever escapes alive," Nix demanded. Her nose whistled as she inhaled. Her eyes taunted me.

"The burning dungeon with the fairies trapped in cages?" I muttered, glancing down at my feet, unable to hold eye contact with the creature.

"How do you know about the flaming pit in the dungeon?"

"We stumbled upon it while fixing the labyrinth."

"You had no right to make alterations to the maze."

"But we were trapped. The air burned my chest and I couldn't breathe. I had to get out of there somehow."

"No one, absolutely no one, can retain knowledge of the pit." The monster paused, seeming almost human for a moment, then continued, "the flaming pit will remain a secret."

I swished spit in my mouth and tried to clear the lump in my throat, but couldn't. I glanced over at the twins huddled together in a corner, sobbing uncontrollably.

"We cannot bear this pain. We are morphing into stone," Puck said, wiping a tear from his left cat eye.

"Don't leave me here," I pleaded.

"We can't stay here like this. Fear and pain

make the uranium too toxic. We will die if we don't morph."

Then, in a swirl of dusty air, Puck and Portia transformed into marble statues. I have to admit a twinge of jealousy nipped my insides. I wished I could just morph into stone anytime I felt pain, anytime guilt washed over me like flood waters. Looking at the twins' petrified faces made me want to break down and sob so I looked away. I latched my eyes onto Nix, but I couldn't bear to look at her, either. Staring ahead, I bent my knees and pressed my weight into my sneakers to hold my legs steady. If I passed out, I'd never regain consciousness.

The truth was I had no solution. No exit strategy. No real hope of ever leaving Pluto alive. I tried to think of Venus. Fiddling with the crystal in my pocket, I waited a moment for a mental picture to develop, for shapes and colors to form. Nothing. I tried again. Slowly, a blurry image seeped into my mind, like a TV screen with the cable disconnected. The murky picture stood in stark contrast to the glistening scenery of Venus. Again, I tried to paint a clear mental image of the beautiful planet. Instead, a bleak scene grabbed hold of me. I flashed back to the sensation of drowning in the ocean as my head grew heavy and my breathing shallow. The steely feeling of guilt sliced me to pieces. I would rather cut off my right thumb with a hacksaw than succumb to more of this torture. Why couldn't I shake the negative feelings?

Popping my stinging eyelids open, I stared intently into Nix's puffed eyes. I couldn't be certain, but I sensed our thoughts linked together. Could Nix read my mind? Was I peering into the head of Nix, adopting her pain and fear? I tingled, believing that the muddled scene in my head belonged to Nix. Maybe in this wretched cave-maze, I was developing telepathic powers, connecting mind to mind with another being. At that exact moment, the monstrous creature averted her eyes, perhaps grasping our connection, unable to feign courage. She could no longer hide her fear behind angry words.

I broke the silence. "Why don't you direct your anger at Danko? Why torture me and the twins?"

"I shall not betray Danko, the supreme ruler of Pluto. I say you must reestablish the maze immediately," Nix said.

"Can't you think for yourself? The only power Danko wields is the power you give him. I dare you to defy him."

"I have clawed my way up from a lowly peon to a member of Danko's elite circle of guardsmen. Along the way, I edged out Plutonians far stronger and smarter than I, and now you have the audacity to suggest that I turn on Danko." Nix paused taking a deep breath, her nose whistling again. "Forget it."

"You can't trick me. I know your fears," I

bluffed.

"What fears? I fear nothing."

"You fear Danko."

"I respect the master. I have no fear," Nix said, glaring at her pointy metal-tipped boots.

"You can't even look me in the eye and say you're not afraid," I dared.

"Fear is for the weak like earth beings. I am strong and powerful."

"You are a coward, preying on me, a kid, and two innocent Venugans. You are too scared to face Danko."

"I am not!"

"What do you gain in Danko's elite circle? He'll kill you eventually. Don't you know that? You are a servant, not the master."

Nix did not move or utter a word. Had I gone too far? Fear claimed my body, starting in my toes and stretching to my scalp. But this fear was not my own, it belonged to Nix. I knew that now. Her face twitched as she gently tapped her right boot on the concrete slab. I struggled to latch onto her mind, but I couldn't. I looked into her eyes and pleaded, "If you will help us, maybe we can all escape this place."

"No."

"We need you."

"I cannot aid a criminal," Nix replied. "Absolutely not."

"We are not criminals. We're just trying to

escape."

"I cannot be seen assisting the enemy."

I just couldn't give up. I had to convince Nix to join forces with us. "Can't you help us? Together we might defeat him," I begged.

"Then what? I will have nothing. I only know life with Danko."

"But you aren't free. You do whatever Danko asks. You're a puppet."

"I am not," she snipped.

"You must know something about the secret notes."

"What did you say? Did you—" She stopped suddenly. All I could hear was the whistling sound of tiny amounts of air going in and out of her nostrils.

I waited. For what, I didn't know.

Without warning, Nix's grotesque body convulsed uncontrollably, like she was having a seizure. As her limbs quivered, my eyes locked with the vacant glass balls floating in her eye sockets. I said nothing, waiting for Nix to be still. Something had changed in her. I could feel it in every bone in my body. When the shaking stopped, she hesitated and I was sure she would let me go free, but I was dreadfully wrong.

Instead, she reached around her neck, unlocked the copper chain necklace, and with one quick snap, whipped the extended chain at my feet. The clasp locked into the bottom shoelace hole of my right sneaker. Nix ranted, "No one must ever utter those words. I have precise orders to eliminate anyone or anything speaking of the secret notes."

As I bent down to rip off my shoe, Nix pushed me through an opening in the stone walls. I screamed in horror but who could save me?

As if I had bungee-jumped, but without slack in the chain, I bounced upside down, my body whipping around a dark open space. I shielded my skull with my arms not knowing whether I would smash into something. Blood rushed to my head and I gasped for air. While every muscle in my body ached, the pain in my neck and shoulders twisted through me. An eternity passed before my heart and lungs returned to their rightful places. A low humming sound, almost like that of an animal or maybe a machine, reverberated through my ears. How long could I hang upside down? What was the chain attached to? And most importantly, what if my foot slipped out of the sneaker?

With great hesitation, I cocked my head back, stretched my neck, and strained my eyes to see what hummed under me. *Oh please be a swarm of friendly ladybugs!* Immediately, I wished I hadn't looked. Surely, this was the end.

A short distance below me, perhaps two arm's lengths, gigantic serrated blades glided back and forth, mimicking a giant food processor. The shiny silver blades glowed in the blackness sending a cold bolt to the base of my neck. I remembered visiting a recycling plant and seeing furniture and lumber tossed into a grinding pit. If my foot slipped out of the sneaker, I would plummet into chopped oblivion, like a discarded three-legged chair.

I sucked a little air into my compromised lungs, trying to relax, but I had nothing. Even a professional gymnast with chiseled stomach muscles would not be able to reach up and grasp the chain. His foot would slide out of the shoe. What hope did I have? I would spend eternity suspended upside down in some type of time-lock. So, rather than continuing to fight, I surrendered, just as I had in the ocean and in the hot air balloon. I pushed the air out of my lungs with a long gentle exhale and let go...

Promptly, a wave of silver light bounced off my eyes and I remembered my crystal. I slipped my hand in my jeans to make sure it hadn't dropped out of my pocket. Thankfully, the crystal remained cocooned in folds of fabric. At least I had the Aphrodite quartz, if nothing else. I kept my right hand in my pocket, wrapped around the crystal, as I considered an escape plan. With the crystal, I always felt a little braver.

From my upside down viewpoint, I could just make out the jagged granite walls at least twenty feet high surrounding me. Where was I? I tried to create a mental map of every room and space I had seen in the castle, but I just couldn't think. My head throbbed in pain. Because I had to hold on to the crystal in my pocket, my right arm felt heavy like a sack of potatoes. How would I ever escape this pit?

My eyes scanned the walls for something to grasp, but it was so difficult to see. I detected nothing—at least not upside down. I pinched my eyes shut to rest them for a moment and then scanned again, trying to remain positive. From somewhere behind me, a small rock jutted out, but it was like looking in a mirror. Everything was backwards and upside down and crazy. I would need both arms to work up enough speed to swing myself over to the rock. But I couldn't lose the crystal. No. I couldn't risk dropping the crystal. Where could I safely put it? With no other choice, I stuck the crystal in my mouth and clenched my teeth.

Just then, a burst of warm energy pulsed up my throat, and down my nasal canal, easing my pain. I could breathe, although I was dangling upside down. Next, I felt a gentle swish of warm air blow the wax right out of my ears. My eyes were working much better now, as if I wore night vision goggles. And, despite a keen sense of smell, the lingering metallic odor no longer sickened me. Somehow the crystal heightened my senses. I had no other explanation.

Breathing slowly and deliberately with my arms hanging loosely, I allowed the oxygen to flood my body. The humming of the blades no longer distracted me. Hanging upside down no longer distracted me, for that matter. It was as if I floated above myself. I felt at peace and yet strong in my resolve to escape Pluto and rescue the other trapped beings.

I then realized I was not alone. Two amplified voices resounded through my head but I recognized neither one. They were male voices. One spoke in a calculated manner like a person paid to give speeches. The other voice was more animated, quicker. I listened intently to the hushed conversation, trying to determine where the speakers were located, who they were, and what they knew.

"Danko will never unlock these chains. He will never release us. He despises us both. But whom does he despise more—you or me?" the slow speaker whispered.

"We need the secret notes to escape. You know that, Father," the faster speaker said.

"But where are the secret notes? Does anyone know?" the father asked.

"They must be here in the castle," the son answered.

"I suppose you are right. Perhaps if we had the crystal we would find the notes," the father said.

I jiggled the crystal in my mouth and continued to listen, holding my body perfectly still to avoid detection.

"What kind of crystal is it?" the son asked.

"Something extraordinary. I have heard the guards boast of its power to control other planets."

"I should have guessed my tyrant of a brother would want total control of the universe."

Brother? The speaker was Danko's brother. That must be the brother from Maldek the snake spoke about. I strained my ears to listen but it was difficult to make out their words. And then complete silence. The kind of eerie quiet like when you wake up in the middle of the night and everyone in the house is sleeping. The grinding blades no longer hummed. Tilting my head back so far that my body nearly hung in a 'J' position, I gasped at the gaping hole below the now stationary blades. I could only imagine how far I would drop through that hole if my foot slipped out of the shoe. I swished the crystal against the roof of my mouth with my tongue and prayed I would wake up from this nightmare.

At the blurred edge of my vision, I thought I detected movement creeping along a wall behind me. Yes. I was sure of it. Something phlegm-colored slithered along the rocks.

The snake had returned.

Maybe it was just a hologram. I didn't dare call out to her because I could not attract attention. Her graceful movement along the rugged stones prompted envy to bubble from within me. I wished I could slink out of danger at will like a snake. I was certain she would slither up to the top of the copper chain and release me. She wanted those secret notes badly. And she needed me or at least she said she did. She must have been making her way across the rocks and then upward to the chain support. She would set me free. I was quite certain of it.

As she pulled further and further away from me, however, a knot of disappointment twisted in my stomach. I couldn't imagine her leaving me in such a dangerous position. If it weren't for the fact that she had a keen sense of vibrations I might have thought she didn't realize I was dangling upside down. But she knew it. She deliberately passed me. We were not allies and, if I ever escaped, I would not trust her again.

Still unable to take my eyes off of her, I watched her glide across the rocks, becoming smaller and smaller as the distance between us grew. Then she crawled out of my range of vision.

Without warning, the blades shifted below me angling downward, as if they were preparing for lunch. I studied the blades, wondering if I were to fall onto them, could I latch onto something before I plunged through the gaping hole. I supposed they were much too slippery for that. But in my keen assessment of the blades I noticed a reflection, the gleaming reflection of Danko's brother and father and maybe even Nix. I'd have to wait until the third figure turned around to see for certain. Yes, unfortunately, Nix had returned.

"I must dispose of you two," Nix stated with an iced tongue.

"We could assist you in your escape. Why not release us?" Danko's father suggested.

"What escape? I am aligned with your mighty son, the Great Danko."

"You stumble in the dark. You have no mind of your own or mastery over your own life," Danko's father replied.

As I listened to them exchange words, I noticed a rather curious event. The three-headed snake was sliding up the rocks now within inches of Nix. As Nix gestured wildly with her arms, the snake slipped into her pocket and retrieved something. I saw the deformed snake clench the jaws of her middle mouth around a silver object and then slowly slide toward Danko's father.

Nix did not appear to suspect anything as she continued to rant. "You two cannot remain on Pluto. Danko has demanded the extermination of his father, Lord Kipp and his brother, Astra."

"Extermination? You treat us like termites."

"The pulverizer is fully operational," Nix stated. "Lord Kipp, you can go first."

"Tell Danko to come and exterminate us himself. He must send a feather-brained robot to perform his unseemly deeds."

I could see the snake sliding behind Nix and unlocking the chains of both prisoners. Danko's father continued to defy Nix and she seemed unable to lose the argument. I wondered whether Danko's father and brother knew they were officially free. A moment later, my question was answered.

Lord Kipp whacked his arm into Nix's back, pushing her off the ledge. Shrieks of terror reverberated through the dungeon as she plummeted through the cavernous hole, her silvery gown floating above her head on the way down. I suppose I should have been happy that an enemy was defeated. But I wasn't. I honestly felt sorry for her. Nix had surrendered all control over her life and let Danko make decisions for her. She became nothing but a robot.

I thought about my own situation. If Danko's father could kill Nix, what would stop him from killing me too? He and his son would do anything to take the crystal and I couldn't have that.

Promptly, the blades angled up toward the ceiling and I could no longer see the snake or Astra and Lord Kipp. I couldn't hear them either, despite my extrasensory hearing. Had they left the dungeon?

Above me somewhere, but out of my range of vision, I could hear the chinking sound of someone winding my chain. Could it be Puck? It definitely wasn't Portia. She didn't do anything on her own. Or maybe the three-headed snake had come back to save me. She might have retrieved the key from Nix's pocket and returned.

Slowly, with a steady churning sound, the copper chain lifted my limp body toward the stone walls Nix had shoved me through. I bent my wrists and loosened my arms, ready to protect my head should I smash into a rock on the way up. I hoped my sneaker was tied tightly.

Up.

Up.

Up.

I could almost touch the wall now. Just a few more feet to go.

"Thank you?" I whispered, through clenched teeth, careful not to swallow the crystal.

No reply.

My rescuer must not have been able to hear me over the cranking sound of the winding chain. I pulled the Aphrodite quartz out of my mouth and squeezed it tightly in my fist. "Thank you for saving me," I called out clearly.

No reply.

I began to get nervous. Could it be one of Danko's guards? A friend of Nix? Maybe it was Danko himself. As I approached the gap in the walls, I could make out grunting sounds.

"Portia, is that you?"

…Another grunt. Who was I about to come face-to-face with?

"He is within reach," I heard Lord Kipp say in his slow, deliberate way. "I shall pull him out now."

CHAPTER 14
Reunited

My heart pumped against my rib cage. Although I could not see them yet, Danko's father and brother were perched above me, winding my flailing body, ready to seize the Aphrodite quartz. No way were they getting it now. I cupped my fist over my mouth and slipped the crystal under my tongue. I would not be able to speak clearly with my tongue pressed against the back of my teeth, but the crystal would be secure. That's all that mattered.

As I reached the opening, I stretched my arms forward and grabbed hold of a pitted slab of stone. I still couldn't see Lord Kipp and Astra, but I sensed they were only feet away from me. Their hot stinky breath confirmed it.

Hoisting myself through the opening, I yanked my right foot out of the sneaker and plopped my weary body onto concrete slab. I realized I was in the exact spot where I stood when Nix pushed me into the void. I would be more cautious this time. A tangle of dread twisted in me as I imagined them snatching the Aphrodite quartz and pushing me into the void. I pinched both eyes shut waiting for the blood to circulate through my veins. I couldn't face them yet, but the stench of their breath was difficult to ignore.

188

Gently tapping the Aphrodite quartz with the underside of my tongue, I popped my eyes open to find myself staring at two male beings, each at least six feet tall. I questioned whether they were related to Danko as neither one of them resembled him in the least. Their skin appeared smooth, not potholed with oozing sores like Danko's. In fact, their blue-tinged skin was more similar to Nix's than Danko's. The older-looking one, Lord Kipp, wore his ink black hair parted on the left side with a low pony tail. His round mud-brown eyes blinked obsessively as if flecks of dirt were trapped under his eyelids. A slender pointed nose dominated his face, giving him an almost regal quality. Danko's brother, Astra, had a chubbier face but the same round eyes and pointed nose. Clumps of frizzy black hair skimmed his shoulders. Both of the men wore tattered midnight blue capes cinched at the waist by a silver cord. The capes draped over most of their bodies with only their gnarled hands and silver metal boots peeking out.

I held the crystal tucked under my tongue.

"Who are you?" Lord Kipp asked, as he stretched to unhitch the chain from a bracket notched in the granite.

"My name is Jack," I said, pronouncing my words slowly as if faking an accent, careful not to swallow the crystal.

"I thought you would be Michael."

"Michael? I have a brother named Michael.

Why would you think my name is Michael?" I asked, forgetting the crystal could slip out of my mouth if I weren't careful.

"The boy hiding in the room upstairs said his name is Michael. He told me he is searching for his younger brother."

I thought of Michael. Could my brother be somewhere in the castle? Was it possible he visited Pluto in a dream just as he visited Venus? The idea seemed crazy, but then again everything about the last few days was crazy. If Michael were in the castle, was he trapped? Danko said he would get even with me. I could feel my chest muscles tighten with anger. Then I just felt numb, defeated.

I stared blankly at Lord Kipp. "Can you help me?" I begged. "I think the earth being you speak of is my brother."

"Could be."

"Was he okay? How did he look? I need to find him and get out of here." As I spoke I could hear the crystal rattling in my mouth, but I didn't care.

"I did not see him. I merely heard his voice through the floorboards." Lord Kipp leaned toward me and I pulled back. "I cannot help you. We must bid you farewell before we are all captured." I watched Lord Kipp and Astra disappear between two smooth stone walls in the labyrinth.

Still pressing the crystal under my tongue, I cocked my ears. I couldn't help but think he and

Astra were devising some horrid plan as they left me. Did they know I had the crystal? They spoke of it in the dungeon. A moment later my question was answered.

"Why didn't you take the Aphrodite quartz?" screamed in my ears. Did Astra's mind connect with mine or did he speak out loud?

"We cannot obtain it by force," Lord Kipp rasped.

"I apologize, Father. It's just I think the crystal is more useful in our hands than in his."

"You cannot confiscate the crystal."

"But I cannot wait any longer," Astra griped.

"You must. Perhaps the earth boy will locate the notes with the crystal and—. "

Lord Kipp's words broke off, leaving me to ponder who or what halted his speech. I realized it was more difficult to distinguish Lord Kipp's echoing words as the distance between us grew. Still, I thought it was strange he stopped mid-sentence, like he stepped off a cliff. Then I heard them. The clicking footsteps of one of Danko's guards.

As the tapping sound of the boots grew louder, I scanned the walls for a hiding spot. Nothing. Should I get down in a crawling position? Maybe the guard was searching for someone else. He could be searching for Michael! I balled up my sweaty palms into fists and held my breath, pressing my back against a stone wall. But now the clack of the boots was not as loud. I had escaped notice. I let out a big puff of air and waited. I could make out voices on the other side of the wall.

"You must give me the chain. You must. Danko said he wants the chain. So give me the chain," a male voice demanded.

"Tell him to retrieve it," Lord Kipp snapped.

"He needs the chain now. Right now."

"Why?"

"He needs the chain. He said if you don't give me the chain, he will torture me. So give me the chain," the stranger demanded, his voice cracking.

"I shall not," Lord Kipp stammered.

"Danko is desperate. He will demolish this castle, take it to the ground. Please don't provoke him. Give him what he wants. Please give me the chain," the man begged.

"No. No. No."

"Then I shall take it."

I swallowed hard. The concrete slab beneath my feet trembled, as if there were an underground explosion or an earthquake. But this was not earth. A sense of panic strangled me, squeezing the air out of my chest. I looked down at my bony hands. They were shaking as much from my fear as from the tremors. If the towering granite walls collapsed, I would suffocate under mounds of rubble. I would be buried alive. I dropped to my hands and knees and crawled over to the twins who remained in the same frozen position as when Nix ambushed us.

"Puck! Puck! I need you," I begged, but I did not expect him to come to life. His feline eyes stared into the distance. His shoulders were relaxed with both mutated wings tucked half-way behind his back. His face was so serene, I was sure his upturned lips were smiling. I envied the peacefulness in his body.

"Jack, it's okay. We're experiencing a vibrational shift on Pluto," Puck said, as he morphed into a living, breathing Venugan. Then, as if on cue, Portia transformed her hardened body as well. She always followed her brother's lead.

The three of us remained still while the cement beneath our feet quivered, as if a jack hammer chopped concrete nearby. After the ground stopped convulsing, I held the crystal in front of me. I expected to see chunks of concrete scattered on the ground, but the walls remained perfectly erect. On every wall in all directions, streams of multicolored light created a grid, like a checkerboard. I could not determine the source of the radiating light beams, but felt comforted nonetheless.

"I'm thinking something crazy," I said.

"What?" Puck asked.

"My brother may be in this castle."

"Why would you think that?"

"Danko's father told me. I know he could be lying, he probably is, but I must look for Michael."

"I admire your determination," Puck said.

"Will you come with me?"

"We will. Hopefully there won't be anymore vibrational shifts for a while."

"What was that vibrational shift?" I asked.

"The balance of electromagnetic energy on Pluto is changing rapidly. Sometimes the pressure is so intense the ground quakes."

"But the walls remained standing."

"This time, yes, but you never know." Puck looked over at his sister. "Portia and I have to be careful during vibrational shifts. If we're solid marble during a violent shift, the trembling will shatter us into millions of pieces."

"Is Danko responsible for the shifts?"

Puck shook his head no. "Quite the opposite. The vibrational shifts frighten him because he can no longer control them. Danko blasts ear-splitting sounds through the castle to stifle the shifts, but I don't think he can curb them anymore." Puck paused, "You must locate the secret notes before it's too late."

"Too late?

"Pluto is rotating so quickly that day bleeds into night. We are running out of time."

"What do you mean? Will the castle collapse?"

Puck did not answer. Perhaps he was afraid or maybe he didn't want to frighten me. I honored the silence, reaching into my jean pocket and twirling the crystal between my index finger and thumb. It radiated a warmth that soothed me and for a brief moment, I wasn't scared.

"Let's go back to the zodiac corridor. If Michael is here, he could be in one of those rooms."

"Lead the way," Puck instructed, motioning for his sister to follow.

Using the crystal as a light source, the three of us twisted through the labyrinth and soon arrived back at the starting point. The door knob leading out to the zodiac corridor glimmered with metallic silver. This was the same knob that disappeared when I first entered the room marked 'SAGITTARIUS'. Was I imagining things? I wrapped my fingers around the knob and turned it gently. Then, I slipped into the corridor with the twins following closely behind.

Pinpoints of light squeezed in from the sloped ceiling, but I couldn't see much. The ear-tingling silence bothered me more than anything, as if some creature would pop out and snatch me.

Reluctant to pull the crystal out of my pocket, I groped down the hallway, my breathing becoming shallower with each step. If I circled around the corridor, would I find more doors carved with signs of the zodiac? Would Michael be in one of them? I turned to the right and walked a few more paces. The twins ran ahead.

The next door we stumbled upon had "TAURUS" carved in capital letters with a bull chiseled in the wood just below it. I fumbled with the brass knob and opened the door. The room appeared small, about the size of a bathroom. Using the violet streams of light from my Aphrodite quartz as a guide, I examined every crevice in the room. No sign of Michael or the secret notes. The room was bare except for a small desk up against the back wall. No chair, just a desk. I pulled open the drawers, peering inside them. Maybe Michael left a message. No. The drawers were empty. I stepped back into the corridor. Up ahead, I could make out a glistening brass knob in the dim lighting.

"The door says Virgo," Puck called out, louder than he should have.

"Is it locked?"

"Yes, but I hear movement."

I scrambled toward the door. Could Michael be hiding in the Virgo room?

"Michael?" I whispered into the door frame.

"Jack?" a voice said from behind the door.

My heart nearly popped out of my throat. "Open the door."

"It's locked."

I couldn't stop shaking as I wrestled with the knob. It wouldn't budge. I pulled the Aphrodite quartz out of my pocket and slid it across the knob. Purple streams of light bounced off the brass and then a popping sound echoed through my ears. I tried the knob again and this time it opened. I stuffed the crystal back in my pocket, drew in a deep breath, and pushed the door open a few inches. The door made a loud creaking sound. I slipped inside the room leaving the twins in the corridor.

Glancing around the dark space for my brother, I could make out a figure about the same height and build as Michael in the shadows. Was I dreaming? Was he just an illusion? A hologram? Michael reached for me. He felt warm and alive and that was good enough for me. We squeezed each other, neither of us saying a word, both afraid to let go.

"I thought I'd never see you again. I miss you so much," Michael whispered. "I've been searching for you, stumbling through strange mazes in the darkness."

"I miss you too," I said, letting go of his arms, "but we can't just hang out. We have to find the secret notes before Danko captures us and the castle collapses."

"How? This castle is huge. I don't know how I found this room or where I am."

"Have you heard anything about the secret notes? Any riddles?" I asked, crossing my fingers in the darkness.

"Funny you say that, I did hear something," Michael said, "I overheard cave troopers whistle a rhyme—almost like a song."

"What did they say?"

"Let me think, something about the notes and the number twelve."

"Think hard."

Michael lifted his head as if the answer were written on the ceiling. I didn't want to say anything and confuse him. "Wait. I remember it," Michael blurted.

"Tell me. Tell me," I begged.

**"The notes you cannot shelve,
They are stuck within the twelve."**

"Twelve? Twelve what?" I asked. "What could twelve mean? Twelve months in a year? Twelve apostles?"

"Twelve could be anything," Michael added. "Twelve eggs in a dozen? Twelve grades in school?"

Numbers swirled through my head, moving backwards and forwards. I could see twelve numbers on a clock, but time was different on Pluto. I stuffed my hand in my pocket and twisted the crystal between my right index finger and thumb. The number twelve spun rapidly through my head, up and down, in and out. It must mean something. And then the answer hit me.

"The zodiac!" I blurted out.

"You think the number twelve is the zodiac?"

"The notes could be in the zodiac corridor somewhere, nestled under a brick in a box."

"Why a box?"

"The secret notes are in a box, according to a riddle I heard. They're also in a toxic stew, in perfect form, or something. I can't remember. I wish I had written down all of the riddles I've heard."

"If they're in a toxic stew, they must be in the dungeon with the flaming pit. That air is barely breathable," Michael groaned.

"I thought they might be in a box in the stone labyrinth."

"Where?"

"My friends and I moved walls in a stone labyrinth. You might have traveled through it."

"Moved walls? How?"

"With my crystal."

"You have a crystal?" Michael blurted. "I had a crystal. Let me see yours."

I pulled the glistening Aphrodite quartz out of my pocket and balanced it in the center of my palm. Michael stared at it for quite awhile. "That's exactly the same as mine. What a coincidence!"

"Not really," I mumbled. "Nothing is a coincidence. Nothing is an accident." I looked away remembering all the pain I caused Michael and my family. I could feel Michael's eyes on me. A single tear dripped onto my hand.

"It might not be important," Michael said, "but I remember something else."

"What?"

"I heard men above me speaking to each other." Michael pointed to the ceiling.

"What did they say?" I asked, assuming he was referring to Lord Kipp and Astra.

"They didn't say anything about the notes, but they repeated a rhyme."

"Can you recall the words?" I asked.

**"With the perfect cord,
balance is restored."**

"What would you do with a cord? Tie something?" I wondered out loud. I remembered the chain I dangled from—how could I forget? Lord Kipp and Astra wanted that chain. Could that be the cord?

"What does a cord have to do with the notes?" Michael asked slowly, sounding confused.

As I listened to his words, my mind exploded. "Wait! What if the cord is not a chain? What if it's a music chord?"

"And the secret notes are music notes." Michael added.

"Exactly. Maybe the box is a music box. It could be hidden in a room out in the zodiac corridor."

"Or in the dungeon with the toxic air."

"Shhh—I hear something," I warned. High heeled shoes clacked against the cement floor outside our room. Clickety-clack. Clickety-clack. Michael and I clung to each other as we listened to the sound of the shoes fade in the distance. When all was silent again, when I felt certain danger had passed, I whispered, "I'm going to get my friends, Puck and Portia. I'm worried about them."

"Hurry back," Michael pleaded. "We don't have much time to find the music notes."

"I'll hurry," I promised. "Wait here. Don't move." Then I stepped out of the room into the corridor. Stupid, I know.

Where were Puck and Portia? Hiding in one of the zodiac rooms? I continued around the hallway to the right, fumbling in the shadows, too frightened to call out the twins' names. I could have taken out my crystal but I didn't. Danko could be lurking behind a door ready to snatch it. I'd keep it safe in my pocket for now.

As I passed each door, I paused, cupped my ear against the wood, and listened for sounds. I heard nothing in Capricorn, Aquarius, Gemini, Libra, Pisces or Cancer. All the doors were locked. I had only one door to go—Scorpio. But something bothered me—the random order of the zodiac signs. Why weren't they in calendar order—Capricorn first and then Aquarius and then Pisces? Before Michael's accident, my mom devoured the daily horoscope. The astrology section was the first thing she read each day. She based decisions on her horoscope, quoting the horoscope as if it were sacred, as if everyone believed in it. What would she think of this mixed-up zodiac corridor?

Standing before the door marked SCORPIO, I considered knocking but chose not to. Someone might hear me. "Puck," I whispered. "Are you in there?"

I could hear Puck's lizard tail thumping against the floor. "Portia and I are both here."

I sighed with relief, closing the door behind me. Dim lighting from the hallway flickered under the door. I could see the twins' bodies stretched across the floor like lions sitting in the shade at the zoo. I pulled out my crystal to get a better look at them in the darkness. "Why are you resting?"

"I injured my paw wrenching the door open," Puck said apologetically. He lowered his head and licked his right paw.

"Did you find the secret notes?" I asked on a whim.

"No, but we figured something out."

"What?"

"The zodiac doors are organized by element. The fire signs are next to each other. So are the water, air and earth signs," Puck said.

"How'd you know that?"

"The name of each element is carved in the lower corner of all the zodiac doors."

That got me thinking. Maybe Danko's castle

needed to be balanced in the four elements. The flame in the dungeon raged out of control. If I extinguished the fire with water, I would clear the toxic air and restore balance. (I wasn't sure how the element "earth" related to the fire pit.) Perhaps if balance were restored, the secret notes would be revealed. I was beginning to think the secret notes were in a music box under the flame. Crazy, I know.

"I need water to put out the flame in the dungeon where the fairies screech," I said.

"Where are you going to get the water?" Puck asked.

"Water flows in the moat around the castle. Maybe we can find a bucket," I suggested.

"A bucket? It will take much more than a bucket of water to douse the flame."

"Is the moat water warm?" I asked, remembering all of the tropical creatures swimming in it.

"Yeah. How'd you know?"

"Pipes must connect the moat water to the flame in the pit. How else would the water be warm enough for tropical fish and crocodiles on Pluto?"

"A loop that transports the water back to the moat?" Puck's eyes widened.

"Just like a solar-heated swimming pool."

"I have never seen pipes connected to the moat, but it's possible."

"I know we'll find water pipes near the

flame," I insisted. "And once the flame is extinguished, we'll uncover the notes underneath."

Puck stared, his mouth wide open. "You have such confidence."

I shrugged. "Are you two coming? I have to get my brother in the Virgo room. Let's go."

"I'm afraid I won't make it." Puck avoided eye contact. "My paw aches and I'd slow you down.

"Lock this door," I instructed. "I'll see you soon." With that, I walked out of the room—more confident than I should have been. Someone had to stop Danko before he controlled everything. As long as I had the crystal, I felt I was up to the task.

I slid down the corridor holding my breath, never quite sure what might jump out at me. When I reached the room marked VIRGO, I let out a big puff of air.

"Michael, open up. It's me, Jack."

No answer.

"Michael, let me in."

No answer.

So I twisted the knob but the door was locked. I could feel my throat tighten as I rapped on the door. "Michael, please."

Desperate, I yanked the crystal out of my pocket and glided it across the knob. No popping sound. The door remained locked. I tried to clear my mind—to be positive. Honestly, I did. Still, the lock didn't budge. I don't know how long I stood outside that door, fighting back the tears. ...I had lost my brother again.

CHAPTER 15
Bad Energy

Part of me thought Michael was searching for the music box. (Maybe he chose to enter the dungeon.) The other part of me, the larger part, knew Michael was captured. There was only one place Danko would take my brother—to the flaming pit. Danko promised he'd get even with me. And he did. I just couldn't erase the gruesome image scraped in my mind. I had to go back to the flaming pit before it was too late.

I sprinted down to the Sagittarius door and found it unlocked. So far, so good. I pressed on the door and entered the stone labyrinth but quickly realized I would need the crystal to see where I was going. I removed it from my pocket and held it at eye level. Tiny rays of violet light squiggled across the stone walls. As I traveled deeper into the labyrinth, the screams from the fairies grew louder and louder. When the deafening sounds grew so strong that I shielded my ears, I knew I had reached the entrance to the flaming pit dungeon.

Gently, I tapped the stone wall with my crystal. The wall retreated immediately, revealing the tortured fairies in cages surrounding a roaring flame. I counted twelve cages and was sure I had solved the mystery of the secret notes.

I would have to jump down.

Slipping the crystal into my jean pocket before hoisting my body onto the stone ledge, I surveyed my surroundings. The ledge, at least three feet by four feet, projected out toward the flaming pit, allowing a view of the entire dungeon. From the ledge, the distance to the ground appeared to be less than ten feet, but my judgment was clouded by the non-stop screeching. I imagined Danko with one eyeball marching toward me, torturing me for the crystal, and then hurling my beaten body into a cage. I thought of Michael. What did Danko do to him? I pushed that image out of my head.

An eerie silence swallowed up the air as if someone hit the mute button. Soon, the distinct sound of flapping wings echoed through the cave. I strained my eyes to see the birds. Where did they come from? And where were they going? More and more flying creatures whizzed through the air, flying low, unfazed by the dim light. But birds don't fly at night. How could these birds see? Hundreds, thousands of birds circled over the silent fairies and then zoomed toward me, like fighter planes on the attack. When the legion of birds flew within ten feet of me, I knew they were not birds. They were blood-thirsty bats preparing to feast on me.

Still perched on the ledge, I tucked my head, arms and legs under my torso. The bats dove straight into my balled up body, nibbling on my neck. The plucking became so painful that I had no choice but to jump down into the pit with the caged fairies.

Squatting in a sprinter's position, with my weight pressed in my toes, I slipped my right hand into my jean pocket but couldn't feel the Aphrodite quartz. Where was the crystal? I had it a few minutes ago in the labyrinth. Panic smothered me like a blanket. I had to retrieve the crystal.

Bats continued to remove little chunks of skin at the nape of my neck. I tried to inhale deeply, to filter out my fears, but my chest clumped up. The sound of flapping wings whistled in my ears. Again, I slid my fingers into my pocket. This time the crystal jostled from inside a crease of fabric, awakening my numb body. I twisted the crystal in my pocket with a new confidence. And then, without a second thought, I jumped more than ten feet into the pit.

My weary eyes, stinging with smoke and tears, failed me and I smashed my skull into a rock. I lay there for some period of time—I don't know how long—with pain shooting through my head down to my ankles. I might have blacked out. When I gazed up at the orbiting bats, they were spiraling higher and higher, the beating sound of flapping wings growing fainter and fainter. Where did the bats go? Did it really matter? I had to find Michael and get out of there. But I couldn't see much.

I knew I could never crawl to the flaming pit with such blurred vision. Recalling that holding the crystal in my mouth heightened my senses, I pulled the Aphrodite quartz out of my pocket and placed it under my tongue.

Ahh… much better! Now I could see!

The crystal seemed to purify the air as it entered my throat making it a little easier to breathe. Not much, just enough to make me think I had a chance.

I could see the fairies glaring at me. Their laser eyes drilled two dozen holes in my back. Did they believe I would save them? Did they somehow blame me? Their screeching had grown louder and more desperate. Who else might be watching me? I looked around.

Someone I recognized teetered on the ledge above me… I knew those blinking eyes. Lord Kipp had made his way through the labyrinth to the edge of the flaming pit. Did he see Michael? I pretended not to notice him, averting my eyes and using only my heightened peripheral vision. Lord Kipp inched along the ledge, and in doing so, slowly emerged out of the shadows with the light cast by the fire.

With the crystal pinned under my tongue, my vision, was so clear, so exact, I thought I was wearing magnifying glasses. I could make out tiny rips on the sleeves of his gown as well as frayed threads at the ends of his silver braided belt. Did he come to warn me of something? Or was he preparing to attack? I looked away in fear.

"Astra, what is that?" Lord Kipp shrieked

from the ledge.

I hadn't seen Astra. I glanced up at the ledge again, startled to see Astra standing an arm's length away from his father. Where was he hiding before? Lord Kipp had turned his left shoulder and was pointing to a gaping hole between Astra's eyebrows. I gasped in sheer terror as dozens of white maggots crawled out, clumped together in a stew of mucous.

"They're chewing me, Father. Stop them, please. I can't bear it," Astra screamed. The sound of his voice echoed through the dungeon.

With one quick thrust, Lord Kipp pressed his crooked fingers against Astra's forehead, as if to stop the bleeding of maggots. But he couldn't block the flow. Astra's face was a piece of rotten meat as throngs of maggots crawled across his forehead.

"My hands! My hands!" Astra yelped, stretching his arms out in front of his face.

I looked at his hands, watching Astra ball his crooked fingers into fists and fling them in the air. I thought he might fall down from the ledge, but he didn't. He held on as cockroaches the size of golf balls climbed out of his knuckles one by one. The roaches, with green pop-out eyes and slits for mouths, marched up the sleeves of his gown and out of my view.

"Father, I can't do this. The bugs are hatching. The bugs that have chomped on our flesh for eons are hatching," Astra cried out in hysterics. "I would sooner hurl my body into that flame than endure this torture one moment longer."

Astra dropped to his knees, slumped over, and nearly fell off the ledge. Because his forehead pressed against his kneecaps, I could no longer see the gushing maggots, but I knew they were still erupting from under his skin as blobs of maggot goop dripped onto the ledge. The cockroaches were slicing tiny holes in his gown and trampling up and down his back and legs. There appeared to be no end to the stampede of creatures.

The skin on my back and shoulders itched so intensely, I longed to scratch until blood trickled down my arms. I thought back to the insects I encountered when I first arrived on Pluto. Could they have laid eggs in my skin? I suppose anything was possible on Pluto, but the mere thought of bugs crawling out of my body curdled the juice in my stomach like cottage cheese. But maybe these creatures hatched and simply wanted to escape Astra's body. I stroked the Aphrodite quartz and hummed softly.

And then, without warning, a stream of multicolored glowing ladybugs swooped down to the ledge from somewhere above me. With my heightened vision, I could see their tiny mouths almost upturned into smiles. As if prancing to the beat of a silent drum, all of the bugs, the cockroaches, the maggots and everything else, swarmed together in unison with the stream of ladybugs leading the parade. Lord Kipp was hunched over stroking Astra's back when the bugs did their exit dance. As soon as the bugs lifted off his skin, Astra stopped howling in pain. The gaping holes which blanketed Astra's hands and face melted together as if someone hit the rewind button. No sign of the bug attack remained. Both Astra and Lord Kipp, clearly still in shock, looked out at the flaming pit with glazed eyes and gaping mouths. My eyes met Astra's but I turned away. Maybe I should have said something, but I chose not to.

"Jack," someone whispered so softly I thought I was hearing things. "Help me. I'm stuck. My skin—" The voice broke off.

"Michael?"

I didn't hear a response although with the crystal in my mouth, I should have heard something. I heard nothing.

"Michael, I'll get you out. Don't worry." The words poured out of my throat as if someone else were speaking for me. What would make me think I could defeat Danko?

I now believed the secret music notes as well as my brother were hidden near the flame. Maybe Michael reached the notes before me only to be captured by Danko's troops. I would be walking into the same trap. As the poisonous air thickened, even with the crystal pinned under my tongue, I struggled for oxygen. If I were going to make it out alive with my brother, I needed a strategy and I needed one fast.

I sketched out a broad plan in my mind. I would find a water pipe and extinguish the flame, then rescue Michael. Executing the plan would prove difficult, though. The intense heat from the fire already had chafed the skin on my arms and neck. Once I reached the flame, the crackling embers would scorch my hair, my face, and my arms if I got too close. And there was something peculiar about this fire. I couldn't quite identify what it was, but the flame burned so hot and so harshly, I feared my skin would melt before I reached my brother.

I crouched down on my hands and knees and crept like a reptile to the torch in the center of the room. Spirals of smoke billowed upward, casting off a wretched burnt chemical odor. My lungs, so weak from sucking in toxic air, were shutting down. Everything in my weary body was shutting down. *Keep going. Don't stop. Your brother needs you. Puck and Portia and the fairies need you.* I pressed my chin against my chest, struggling to suck in the smallest amount of oxygen, but the air was too poisonous even with the crystal.

Inching closer to the flame, I could see the fire raged from within a dark metal urn with two twisted handles on either side. The urn, at least four feet high with a large round base, appeared quite heavy. I hoped I wouldn't need to move it.

I was almost there now. The twisted handles were shaped like snakes with their tongues licking the flames. But where was the water pipe? It had to be connected to the urn because the moat water was warm. It was just a matter of finding the pipes. I flicked the crystal under my tongue, hoping to latch onto the image of a water pipe.

Soon, the glow of a copper hose caught my eye. I pinched my eyes closed, hoping the hose wouldn't burn me, as I gently touched it with my right pinky finger. The copper casing was quite hot, but not so hot that I wouldn't be able to grab it. I assumed the cold water circling in the moat cooled the hose slightly.

I could not locate the hose connector, but there had to be some way to unleash the water. I clasped the copper hose and wiggled it back and forth with both hands. It wouldn't snap. Again, I twisted the metal hose, but it did not crack. I was becoming more desperate with each attempt. The water was so close, yet I couldn't get at it. Maybe I could use the crystal to puncture a hole in the hose.

I pulled the Aphrodite quartz out from under my tongue and pressed it against the copper. I squeezed my burning eyes shut and dreamt of water gushing out of the hose. Water pouring onto the flame. Water cleansing the air in the pit. A low hum reverberated through my right hand, but I didn't release my tight grip. A drizzle of water dripped onto my wrist. The crystal melted a hole in the copper hose!

Rapidly, the trickle gushed into a steady stream as the hole expanded. Pressing my left thumb partially over the hole, I sprayed water at the crackling fire, but the flame roared. It raged as if I doused it in gasoline. This fire was unlike anything I had seen on earth. Was this a trick flame, like birthday candles that won't go out? I jammed the crystal back into my pocket for safekeeping.

More and more water surged out of the copper hose, as the water pressure increased and the hole expanded to the size of a baseball. I struggled with the hose, battling for control, my sopping wet sneakers sliding on the concrete floor. The water inched up my feet, soaking my ankles. I knew I had no time to battle the flame— I had to get out of there! But where was Michael?

Promptly, a low rumble resounded through the cave, like a subway train. Another vibrational shift? Would I be trapped under pounds of rock, unable to move, slowly suffocating? I struggled to keep my balance, pulling my water-drenched feet apart and locking my shivering knees. The stone walls surrounding me shook violently, muffling the fairies' shrieks. Instinctively, I drew my arms to my head, fearing a slab of crumbling rock would smash into my skull. I needed someone to help me, to make everything okay, to wake me up from this nightmare.

I lifted my eyes and peered at the ledge where I had last seen Lord Kipp and Astra. Lord Kipp stood with his arms stretched out like a preacher. He was chanting something in a foreign language that Astra seemed to understand, but I didn't.

"Help Me!" I screamed, but I was only talking to myself. Anyone who could possibly help me was gone.

The vibrating concrete beneath my feet grew still and the dungeon grew quiet. I wanted to inhale deeply, but my lungs were crippled. By now, the frigid water was licking my knees. I searched the walls for an opening, a crack, anything that would offer me hope of escaping the flooding water. Nothing. I felt so alone yet somehow knew I wasn't. A dark presence filled the space around me. Someone or something other than the fairies lurked in the air, in the water, saturating the dungeon, although I couldn't see it.

I reached into my pocket and caressed the Aphrodite quartz, seeking some type of positive energy. Closing my eyes, I remembered the feeling in the ocean as the waves sucked me under. I didn't want to fight anymore. I just wanted to surrender. Even the fairies had stopped screaming. Maybe they had given up hope too.

"Jack! Jack! Over here!" a voice startled me. The words came from behind me, somewhere on the right hand side. I turned around, but no one was there.

"Michael, where are you? I can't see you in the smoke."

"I'm trapped in a cage about twenty feet behind you. My cage is filling with water—it's up to my waist."

I turned around and waded through the water, but I couldn't find Michael's cage. I studied the fairies' cages, searching for Michael in between them. The fairies wrapped their fingers around the copper bars and clung to the tops of their cages, their voices silent. I couldn't look in their eyes. I had caused the flood and they knew it. Still, I didn't feel anger coming from them, just sadness.

"Michael, I don't see you. Where are you?" My heart thumped against my ribs. With water gushing in at this rate, we would drown in less than ten minutes.

"I'm over here. Ten feet away from you. On your left," Michael's voice quivered.

Following his voice, I trudged through the water, now up to my belly button. I stuck my shivering hand into my pocket and clasped the crystal between my index finger and thumb, fearing my crystal would float away. I was preparing to place the crystal under my tongue when, without warning, a sharp voice boomed through the pit, as if connected to a microphone. "How dare you cross me?"

This was the end. Danko had come to collect

the crystal and slowly torture Michael and me. At least I would not die alone.

"Let Michael go free. If you release him, I'll give you the crystal," I bargained. "You can have me. Let him go."

A clinking sound clamored in my head, like rattling coins in a jar. I knew it was Danko but I couldn't see him because my eyes stung like I had soap in them. I tried to splash water on my eyeballs, but I still couldn't see. I could hear something—a whirling sound; the clinking had stopped.

When I finally opened my eyes, I observed Danko grasping the end of a copper chain and swinging though the dungeon. I now knew why he insisted on getting the chain. He had planned this whole scenario. He knew I would eventually find Michael and, like an expert chess player, he stayed a few moves ahead of me.

Hanging from the chain several feet above the fire, Danko was protected from both the flooding waters and the raging flame.

Unfortunately, I was not.

I couldn't help but stare at the purple pus oozing from the empty socket where I had ripped his eyeball out. I half-expected a trail of termites to emerge from the hole. Danko's remaining eye locked with mine, stabbing me, daring me to try again. But he was wasting away and appeared completely insane. He wore an oversized silver jacket, which rather than puff him up just made him look like a kid in his father's clothes. A fluorescent green fluid poured out of the holes scattered across his face. He had nothing to lose—that much I knew. If he didn't get his bony hands on my Aphrodite quartz, he would die.

"Give me that crystal!" Danko shrieked, his slender sickly arms poking out from under the shiny jacket, clutching the chain.

"No!" I snapped back. "I will not! Drain the water in this cave."

"You and your pitiful brother will drown here if I don't get that crystal," Danko snickered. "Or you can meet the same fate as those traitor twins!"

"What did you do with Puck and Portia?" My heart dropped to my stomach. I struggled to swallow over the golf ball-sized lump in my throat.

"I banished those mental midgets to an eternity of misery," Danko's eyes widened. "They betrayed me and now they shall circle round and round on a carousel forever."

"The carousel outside? In the amusement park?"

"There's no amusement. It's not a merry-go-round—more like spinning platform of torture."

"What are you doing with Michael?"

"Your brother is drowning. He will be dead before he can inhale five more breaths."

"Release him!" I demanded, still shaking on

the inside. "You have lost all your power. You can't even save yourself."

"I can do anything I want. If I want the water to recede, it will obey me," Danko belted out as the water gurgled. A violent sucking sound echoed through the pit as the water level dropped to below my knees. "Now give me that crystal!"

"Michael! Michael! Where are you?" The goose-bumped skin on my arms, neck and legs itched. Why wasn't Michael answering? Promptly, as if a dam broke, water gushed into the cave again.

"How are you at catching barracudas with your bare hands?" Danko taunted. "Your brother makes a delicious feast for my hungry boys." Danko gestured toward a hole in the ground with his left hand.

I waded through the waist-high water over to the hole where Michael clung to a cage at least two feet below ground level. The water was lapping up against his chin and rising quickly. The barracudas circled around Michael, brushing up close to him. I couldn't bear to look.

"Let him go!" I pleaded, not fearing for myself. "I'll give you the crystal."

Abruptly, the water stopped gushing, as if someone twisted a giant knob and shut it off. "Back off, Danko!" a husky female voice called out from behind me. The voice belonged to the three-headed snake.

"Who are you?" demanded Danko, still clinging to the copper chain, but now visibly shaking.

"You know who I am," the snake answered.

"No, I don't."

"I'm the snake from Maldek."

"I don't know any snakes from Maldek. Where's Maldek?" Danko questioned, but it was obvious he knew.

"You know who I am. My name is Hydra, you lying monster."

My eyes strained to see Hydra. Where was she? I could hear her voice coming from somewhere near the flame.

"Where are you?" Danko asked, fear scratched in his voice.

"I'm over here, coiled around the copper hose. I have stopped the water from flowing. Now you will listen to me, Danko!" the snake demanded.

"I don't fear a little worm," Danko cried out, his voice breaking up.

"You and your radioactive experiments destroyed my whole family on Maldek. You turned the soil toxic, the air, everything we ever knew. You must pay for killing all the snakes. For destroying my planet. Maldek is nothing but asteroid chunks because of you!"

"But you told me to fight my brother."

"I thought you would lose," Hydra hissed. "I concealed the crystal in Astra's shield. He should have won."

"But my father hid the crystal."

"You are mistaken," Hydra boasted.

"What?" Danko shrieked. "I lured my father and brother here; chaining them to a ledge in a treacherous pit because I believed my father wanted me to lose the swordfight."

"You were mistaken," Hydra repeated.

"What are you saying? My father did not want Astra to win over me?"

"Who cares? I wanted you to lose," Hydra jeered. "But you won."

"Father! Father! Proclaim before these fools my superiority. I am the better son, am I not?" Danko bellowed. "I am more cunning. Tell them."

Silence.

I looked up at Lord Kipp and Astra still perched on the ledge. I couldn't get a read on them. Were they trapped and frightened with no way to climb down? Or were they just spectators with ringside seats to Danko's fight? Lord Kipp appeared to be a mannequin; his blue skin glowed like waste from a nuclear experiment. He said nothing, his eyes glazed over staring out at the flame. I thought he would be happy to see that Astra wasn't suffering anymore. Instead, he appeared to be in a trance, as if his mind were a million miles away. Astra, in contrast, looked overjoyed. His pudgy face, only moments before the sight of a bug stampede, now glowed like a Venusian's.

Danko broke the silence with a second plea. "Father! I am a genius. Tell them what a child prodigy I was. Tell them how I created brilliant inventions—how I mixed chemical compounds," Danko begged, almost panting. "Soon I will topple my enemies in the Dark Brotherhood and control everything."

I lifted my eyes and fixated on Lord Kipp. The color of his skin transformed from a sickly blue to a fleshy pink as blood slowly bubbled through his arteries and veins. His breathing was measured, shallow at first, and then deeper and deeper with every in-breath. I could make out guttural sounds erupting from deep within him.

"You are not a genius!" Lord Kipp growled. "I am ashamed to be your father, but I blame myself."

"Blame? The snake said you did not put the crystal in Astra's shield. Did you?" Danko asked.

"No, but I could never forgive you for your mother's death. I know you were only days old when she died, but I blamed you nonetheless. Maybe you would not have spent so much time joining forces with the Dark Brotherhood and conducting experiments if I had embraced you."

"Father, tell them I am the grand master."

"I shall never say that. My heart is broken," Lord Kipp whispered. He clutched his chest with his crooked fingers and moaned in pain. His head smacked against the stone wall and then his body slumped into a heap on the ledge. It was Astra's turn to comfort his father.

"Father, tell them!" Danko snarled. "I am superior! Say it! Say it!"

Lord Kipp did not move. He might have had a heart attack or maybe he just fainted. Either way, he was not speaking and neither was Astra.

With no response from his father, Danko pressed the snake for answers, "Why did you want me to mix radioactive elements?"

"I thought you'd blow yourself up long before you could hurt anyone else." Hydra's three heads were bobbing up and down in excitement. "How could I have predicted you would annihilate the whole planet with your nuclear games?"

"Nuclear games? This is not a game, Baby Caterpillar. I am the supreme master of Pluto. Soon I shall dominate the entire universe."

"Rubbish. You are poison for this solar system. As you have destroyed me, you must be destroyed. Look how repugnant I am with three radioactive heads."

"I am a brilliant chemist!"

"You are a coward. I will wait here until you are reduced to dust," Hydra insisted, the venom on her tongues cutting through the thick air.

"You cannot stop the barracudas from

devouring these two earth boys. Jack will give me the crystal and you will lose," Danko screeched.

"Let the boys go," Lord Kipp commanded. "Don't make them pay for what I have done."

"I will not release them until I get the crystal."

"Then I must go. I cannot watch your torture," Lord Kipp said.

"You're not going anywhere, Father. You will watch me crush these two."

No matter what happened to me I had to try to save Michael. I'd sooner die a slow painful death than watch him contend with ferocious barracudas. The time had come to surrender the Aphrodite quartz.

Michael squeaked in a feeble voice, "Jack, they're biting me. Their teeth are gnawing at my flesh. Help me!"

"Stop them, Danko! Stop them now!" I screamed. "Here's the crystal." I reached into my pocket and pulled it out.

With one arm clasping the chain and the other flailing wildly, Danko swung over to me. He dangled several feet above my head.

"Chain be lowered!" Danko demanded. I didn't know whether he was instructing someone above or simply ordering the chain to drop down.

As commanded, the chain dropped. Danko clasped the last few links with his mangled hands. Even more hideous up close, Danko wrinkled his face and let out a snarl as he reached down to grab the crystal. Reluctantly, I extended my arm toward him with the Aphrodite quartz clutched tightly between my fingers. He grabbed for it but missed, swinging past me as a loud thunderous cackle boomed through the dungeon.

"The Aphrodite quartz is mine," Danko growled, swinging toward me again, nearly kicking me in the head as he lunged.

"Take it," I said. "If you free Michael and the others, you can have it."

With one more sweeping motion, Danko dove for my crystal and took hold of it.

"Now I shall rule the universe!" he screamed. "Bow before me, Father and Brother."

I did not take my eyes off Danko. I watched as he retrieved the other crystal, Michael's crystal, from his breast pocket and attempted to connect them. I'm not sure what I expected to see as the twin crystals joined together, but no one could have anticipated what happened next. As the twin crystals touched, they exploded in Danko's hands, spraying shards of rock in every direction.

Boom! Boom!

The violent explosion reverberated through the dungeon. Maybe Danko's negative energy was too much for the crystals. I will never know for certain. What I do know is that the explosion created a chemical reaction in Danko's body, transforming him right before my eyes. First, Danko's body morphed into a hot bubbling liquid, like an ice cube tossed into boiling water. He howled in anguish. Next, his liquefied body transformed into a blue gas. The gas spiraled around the chain and then floated upward in a funnel cloud formation, becoming thinner and thinner until it disappeared. Finally, Danko stopped screaming and there was silence.

CHAPTER 16
The Secret Notes Revealed

It was as if time stopped. I simply could not believe what I had witnessed. For a moment, I forgot about my brother, Hydra, Lord Kipp, Astra, the fairies, everyone. But then, a loud gurgling sound swallowed up the still air. The water began spinning clockwise like a whirlpool, like someone pulled out the drain stop. Within a minute, all of the water in the cave was sucked away. I bolted over to Michael's cage and pried open the lock with my teeth. Michael's frail body shivered violently and I debated whether he had the strength to walk or not.

"You saved my life," Michael whispered.

"I couldn't let the barracudas devour you. I had to surrender the crystal."

"You were willing to give up everything for me. Thank you."

I grabbed under Michael's arms and hoisted him out of the cage. His body flopped against me, but I felt strong, like I could carry him up ten flights of stairs as we ambled across the sopping wet floor. Looking around the dungeon, I noted the fairies still clinging to the tops of their cages, their faces frozen. Hydra remained wrapped around the copper pipe with each of her three mouths grinning. I lifted my eyes to the ledge where I last saw Lord Kipp and Astra, but they vanished and I wondered if they saw what happened to Danko.

I glanced above the snake to the dancing flames in the center of the dungeon. The dazzling fire must have ignited something within me because rather than fear, I felt lighter and more alive. Michael's body no longer weighed me down. Guilt no longer pressed against my shoulders pushing me into the floor. And then the craziest thing started to happen. The color of the fire transformed from red to orange, yellow, green, blue, indigo and finally to the most vibrant shade of violet. The brilliance of the shifting colors reminded me of Venus.

A rumbling under my feet jolted me back to reality. I bent my knees and separated my legs to brace myself, propping Michael's limp body against mine. Within a moment, the shaking quieted and now there was only a slight vibration, like the washing machine on spin cycle. And then, the cave grew still. Strangely still. I inhaled deeply, held the oxygen in my lungs to the count of three, and then let it out.

I thought I heard humming, sounds that were almost human. As the hum grew louder and more melodic, I realized the sounds were coming from the fairy cages. Not words, but sounds. I listened intently. The fairies seemed to be chanting, "*ut, re, mi, fa, sol, la*". Each note resounded through me, healing me, sucking the toxic air out of my cells. I could feel Michael's skin warming against mine as we both listened to the fairies' chants.

Then a curious thing happened. One by one, each of the fairies shape-shifted into a small white bird, scarcely larger than a dove. Each bird passed through the copper wires of its cage and soared up toward the ceiling. As they flew higher and their song grew softer, I couldn't help but feel happy for them—like I released wild birds from a zoo. Celeste never told me her siblings were birds.

"Have you heard that song before?" the snake asked, slithering toward us, her three heads lined up single file.

"No."

"I haven't listened to the sacred music scale since I lived on Maldek," Hydra mumbled. "I forgot how beautiful it is."

"What's the sacred music scale?" I asked.

"Six notes, each with a different frequency. Supposedly, these notes heal damaged DNA, particularly the third note 'mi'."

The snake's words exploded in my head. "The secret notes!" I cried out. "The fairies sang the secret notes!"

Hydra's three heads spun around and around, as if she were dancing. "You released the secret notes," Hydra exclaimed with all three mouths.

"How?"

"When you gave the crystal to Danko and he evaporated, you eliminated Danko's absolute power over the fairies."

"So they started singing?"

"Once Danko was gone, the toxic flame which held the uranium inside the fairies burned pure," Hydra paused, visibly excited by her deductive skills. "With Danko's toxic uranium neutralized, the fairies were afraid no longer. They could sing joyously."

"What do the music notes do?"

"The music reactivates hidden strands of DNA, strands responsible for healing. Why didn't I figure that out before?"

I thought back to all of the riddles. "When I first met you on the roller coaster, you talked about the secret notes in a box. There's no box here," I insisted.

"Maybe it was their voice boxes," Hydra said with a triple grin.

"Maybe." I remembered the riddle about the toxic stew. Michael was right. The fairies were in a toxic dungeon. And there were twelve fairies. Suddenly all of the riddles made sense. So if the crystal led me to the secret notes, was Michael cured? Were hidden strands of DNA is his body reactivated? I couldn't believe it was that easy.

"Will Michael be cured when we return to earth?" I asked the snake.

Hydra turned her three heads away from me. "I cannot say," she mumbled.

"What do you mean? You told me if I found

the secret notes, my brother would be cured. You promised."

"I-I-I was mistaken. I was hoping—I don't know," the snake stammered. Her mouths seemed to contradict each other. "It's possible. Anything is possible."

"Anything is possible if you have the crystal, but I don't."

"Don't give all the credit to the Aphrodite quartz. You were the one who saved Michael in this dungeon, not your crystal," the snake insisted. "And what did I do? I was selfish."

"You saved us all when you stopped the flood in here. You didn't have to do that."

Hydra's body lay flat on the ground with her trio of heads propped up like a pitchfork. Slowly, she twisted her heads into a braid. "I wanted you to find the secret notes because I knew their discovery signaled the end of Danko's rule. I used you. You represented the element earth. Will you forgive me for misleading you?"

"I guess so," I said, trying to hide my smile. I should have been angry. I had been such a fool believing her. But, strangely, I wasn't.

Hydra opened her mouths, each displaying a spoon-shaped purple tongue. Her words poured out in unison, "I have spent my lifetime plotting revenge against Danko for all the harm he did to the snakes of Maldek, for the trauma he caused with his botched scientific experiments. I never meant to hurt anyone else," Hydra whispered. "I only meant to crush Danko, but there is no satisfaction in Danko's destruction. I thought there would be, but I was mistaken."

"What will you do next?"

"I will start anew and not waste the remainder of my life on vengeful pursuits. You will not find me stalking you in the bushes here or on any other planet."

"I'll miss you."

"I must move on," Hydra said as her deformed body morphed into three. Like a stick of licorice pulled apart, her tightly braided heads split into a trio of snakes. Each of the snakes shed its bluish translucent skin, revealing a vibrant coat of silver skin—velvety, not scaly. All three snakes slithered away in a different direction, never glancing back at us, but that was okay with me. I had wavered in my opinion of Hydra, but now I knew she intended no harm. Where would each of the snakes go? I wondered if I would ever know.

I lifted my eyes toward the ceiling. By now, the last of the twelve white birds had flown away. They had discovered a hole in the ceiling of the cave and vanished. Although I no longer could hear their song, I imagined each of them soaring through the sky, releasing every creature Danko had controlled for eons. Suddenly I remembered Puck and Portia.

How did I forget them?

"I have to save the twins," I blurted out loud.

"Your friends in the zodiac corridor?" Michael asked.

"Yeah. Danko captured them. "

"Where are they?"

"On a carousel outside. How do we get out of here?"

"Good question," Michael mumbled under his breath.

I was suddenly aware of the walls surrounding me. I hadn't noticed any doors or windows. But then again I hadn't been looking. I would need a ladder to climb out of the pit. That was assuming I knew where the opening to the stone labyrinth was, which I didn't. And of course there weren't any ladders propped up against the stone. Still, I can't say that I was afraid, because I wasn't. Maybe a little doubtful, but not afraid. Standing next to Michael, speaking with Michael, gave me such a sense of peace I would have traded every Christmas and birthday just to stay there with him.

"Do you think we'll get out of here?" Michael asked.

"We will," I insisted, trying to convince myself. My crystal hadn't been gone twenty minutes and already I needed it. If I still had the Aphrodite quartz in my pocket, I could have repositioned the walls at will. But it was gone.

"If only we had something to scale the walls, some kind of rope," Michael suggested.

I looked all around the cave, dungeon, whatever it was. Then I glanced up. "I have an idea. We can climb that chain," I said, pointing to the copper chain Danko had clutched in his twisted fingers. It appeared to be the same chain that suspended me upside down when Nix shoved me. How was the chain hooked to the ceiling? I supposed if it could bear the weight of Danko, it would hold my brother and me. Did we really have a choice?

"When we reach the top of the castle dome how will we get down?" Michael asked.

"We'll figure that out when we get up there. We've made it this far." I lifted my gaze to the chain swinging before me. "Do you want to go first?"

"If you insist," Michael replied making his way to the chain.

I watched my brother make the climb. He never looked down. He never seemed afraid. He just kept climbing and climbing and soon reached the top. Then it was my turn. I inhaled deeply, grabbed the chain in both fists, and climbed feverishly without looking down. After reaching my brother, I could finally let the air out. With one giant swing, I stretched my right leg through the hole and clawed my way up onto the roof. I plopped down next to my older brother like he was saving me a seat in a movie theater. I had trouble believing we had made it out of

Danko's castle, although we weren't completely free. We still had to find our way from the castle roof to the ground below. And, of course, there was that small detail of figuring out how to return to earth. But all I could think about was Puck and Portia. Were they safe?

Looking out from the castle rooftop, everything on Pluto seemed fresher, cleaner, more inviting. The greenish mist had evaporated, replaced by an almost edible tangerine sky. As I pulled in more and more oxygen, my head got lighter and lighter, making me giddy. I was coming back to life.

"I'm so hungry, I could devour a sack of raw potatoes," I remarked.

"I was just thinking the same thing. I haven't eaten in almost a month," Michael replied. "It feels good to be hungry."

"I don't think they eat food here. We'll have to wait until we get home to pig out."

Michael wiggled his body like he was uncomfortable but said nothing. He just grunted. I couldn't think about it, though. I needed to find the twins.

"Look! There's a super slide!" Michael exclaimed, rising to his feet and gesturing to the left. "We can slide down to the ground."

I slowly stood up, careful not to lose my balance. A few paces away on the roof, a gigantic wavy yellow slide about three feet in width hugged the outer wall of the castle leading all the way to ground level. From my vantage point, it appeared the slide gently tapered off onto a drawbridge. It couldn't be the same drawbridge I crossed in entering the castle because I didn't remember seeing a neon yellow slide. Then again, it was so foggy before, maybe I missed it.

"There's a pile of burlap sacks right here," Michael said. "Want to go first?"

I grabbed a sack, placed it at the top of the slide, and sat down, my fingers clutching the frayed edges of the burlap. Then with one big thrust, I slid down, hooting and hollering all the way onto the bridge. Not to be outdone, Michael crawled onto his stomach and slid down head first, his fingers only lightly touching the edge of the sack.

"Wish we could do that again," Michael squealed as he tossed the sack onto the ground next to his feet.

"Maybe when we get home."

"Maybe," Michael murmured, averting his eyes.

My brother trailed me by several feet as we made our way across the first bridge. In truth, Michael loved aquariums and I shouldn't have been surprised that he wanted to check out the tropical fish in the moat. Still, I couldn't help but wonder if he was stalling, pretending to admire the fish to avoid any discussion of the trip back to earth.

"The crocodiles and barracudas are gone." Michael called out. "These fish are incredible. Look at the purple tail on that one."

"Yeah. Yeah. It's great," I said glancing quickly at the water. "I can't stay. I have to find my friends."

"Did you see the colors on the stained glass windows?" Michael asked. "The castle was so grungy before and now look at it."

I looked back at Danko's castle for all of about five seconds. I had to admit it seemed like something out of a fairytale, like Cinderella would stroll out the front door any moment. But I wasn't about to waste time admiring it.

"The carousel's over there," I said, pointing to the rickety blue and white circular structure I remembered seeing when I first landed on Pluto. "I'll race you."

We zipped across the second bridge neck and neck. Scattered in the field were rides so perfect and gleaming, I would have thought it was an amusement park grand opening. We dashed past a golden Ferris wheel with neon orange passenger baskets and then a red wooden roller coaster, but didn't stop until we reached the carousel. Despite my efforts, Michael edged me out by at least a yard and, bypassing all of the white horses, hopped up on top of Puck. A chipped brass pole pierced Puck's spine, securing him to the platform. My brother grabbed hold of his crippled wings. Puck looked so uncomfortable, his upper lion body balled up and hunched over. He said nothing to us.

The carousel horses were rigid yet lifelike, like they were sleeping with their eyes wide open or, maybe, like they had just died. And then it hit me. These horses had to be Asea's friends. They probably drank Danko's toxic mixture of chemicals and found themselves imprisoned on Pluto. I studied the horses carefully. What appeared to be saddles from a distance were actually chopped wings laying flat on their backs, dingy gray wings. At any moment, I expected one of the horses to speak or at least swish his tail. But there was no movement from the horses.

Where was Portia? If the twins were positioned adjacent to each other, they might not have been so lonely, but Danko would never have allowed that. So I looped around the carousel in search of Portia, knowing she'd be planked down on the opposite side of the platform, unable to see her brother. I was right.

Like Puck, Portia was hunched over, the weight of her body resting on her tail with a tarnished brass pole piercing her back between her wings. Deep frown lines were chiseled into her lion face. She said nothing. But this time, the silence was so deafening, so heavy, thoughts in my head screamed at me. I was the reason she and her brother were being punished. If they hadn't gone into Danko's castle and helped me, they'd be free now.

"Are you okay?" I asked, knowing she wouldn't answer, but somehow feeling better for inquiring. "May I take a ride?"

She didn't reply but her stone exterior felt warmer. I took that as an open invitation and jumped up on her back. We started spinning slowly at first and silently, not making much more than a whoosh sound. I closed my eyes and imagined gliding in the balloon across the lavender-dipped skies of Venus—and for a moment I was, if only in my mind.

"Where are you?" Michael called out, blocked from my view by a giant mirrored support in the center.

"I'm on the other side."

The music started. Only a low hum at first, the music grew louder and louder until my ears overflowed. This was not the annoying pipe organ music played continuously on merry-go-rounds. No this was different—almost like the harmonic sounds chanted by the fairies in the castle. The secret notes.

"There's Puck," a soft voice said, nearly drowned out by the music.

Was that in my head? Or was Portia speaking? I leaned in closer and studied her mouth. I could see Portia struggling to clear her throat as words bubbled up from deep within her, barely audible at first.

"There's Puck," she repeated, her voice strengthening. "We're getting closer to Puck."

And we were. Somehow Portia had freed herself from the pedestal attached to the spinning platform and we were prancing toward Puck and Michael. I wrapped my fingers around the base of her neck and sat up straight watching Danko's castle whirl by over and over again. Making our way between the white wooden horses, we nearly caught up with Puck and Michael, but then Puck released himself from the pedestal and galloped freely on the rotating platform. We were spinning faster now, faster and faster. Soon, the other horses broke free of their rusty poles and shifted to the left, making room for us.

"Puck! Puck! Wait up!" I screamed. His strides were strong and graceful, more like a horse than a lion or reptile. As Portia galloped toward her brother, never quite catching up to him, we seemed to be lifting off the platform. I assumed it was my imagination—but it wasn't.

Suddenly, we were airborne, soaring through a kaleidoscope of geometric patterns in the Plutonian sky. I locked my chin, fastening my eyes to the skies directly ahead, too frightened to look down. How were we flying? Somehow Portia's deformed body had lifted into the air, but how?

The gentle hum of flapping wings reassured me and I began to enjoy the ride. When I peeked down at Portia's back, still clutching her neck, I observed long, translucent silver-painted wings, not the hacked wings she bore for ages. Squeezing her neck a little more tightly, I glanced over my shoulder to see if Michael was riding on Puck's back. He was. Directly behind him, flying in a V formation, were the wooden horses from the carousel ride. Portia noticed them too and circled back toward them, dipping lower then ascending like a kite. I squinted to see the last white horse use a rusty pole to vault into the air, finally freeing himself from Danko's control. My eyes widened as I noticed that each of the horses had sprouted glimmering gem-colored wings— amethyst, ruby red, emerald green, candy orange, ice blue, and diamond white. They soared through the air gaining speed and soon flew past us.

I had no idea where we were going. Back to earth? Back to Venus? I can't say I was worried, because I wasn't. We could have been heading to the Andromeda Galaxy for all I cared. I was free! Free from Danko. Free to be happy with my brother again.

CHAPTER 17
Hello and Goodbye

Wherever we were headed, we were speeding in the direction of the sun which by now was wrapped in an evening orange glow the color of cantaloupe. A warm breeze kissed my skin, radiating through my body, making me feel like I would blow a fuse. I didn't feel dizzy or sick to my stomach, just peaceful. And then the space ride was over. We were definitely on our way down.

"Where are we landing?" I asked.

"You'll see," Portia responded. "We'll touch down soon."

I twisted my shoulders in search of Michael and Puck, but I could no longer see them or the horses for that matter. I then turned my attention to the sights under me. Several hundred feet below us, a raging waterfall cascaded into a blue porcelain lake, shooting white foam into the air. Surrounding the lake were checkered fields of wildflowers with alternating colors of greenish yellow and cornflower blue. Each blue or yellow square appeared as large as a suburban front lawn, but I couldn't be certain from so far up in the sky.

The perfumed smell of flowers, hyacinths or maybe honeysuckle, snuffed out the stench of chemicals that clung to my nostrils on Pluto. After so much time in Danko's castle, I delighted in feeling my chest rise and fall as I inhaled slowly, held my breath to the count of three and then exhaled. The air felt flawless against my skin, neither cold nor hot, like Venus. As we continued to drop, the color of the sky changed to a muted lilac and I began to recognize familiar Venusian landmarks.

"We're coming home!" Portia shouted, nearly jolting me off her back in excitement.

Gliding down slowly like falling leaves, we floated toward the amusement park. Hundreds of Venusians scurried about the park like ants in mounds of dirt. I could hear shouting and laughter and couldn't wait to jump on the rides with my brother. Beyond the three-ringed Ferris wheel, an inflated hot air balloon the color of grape juice stood adjacent to the carousel. We were gaining so much speed, I thought we would clip the top of the balloon as we passed it, but we didn't. We cleared it by at least ten feet, plopping down in a smooth patch of grass between the balloon and carousel. I thanked Portia for the ride and hopped off her back.

I lifted my eyes to the sound of flapping wings above me and watched the first white horse swoop in under the silver canopy covering the carousel and plunk down onto the platform. Then, one by one, the remaining twenty horses landed, their glittering wings catching the sunlight like stained glass. Their thick white coats appeared freshly brushed and their manes smooth, not windblown like you'd expect. As the classical music started, the wooden platform began rotating slowly, about the speed of a baggage claim conveyor belt. There were no brass poles securing the horses to the platform. Poles wouldn't be necessary.

No sooner had the horses landed on the platform, when a group of Venusians dressed in silver togas climbed on them. As I looked more closely, I recognized the Venusians. They were the fairies on Pluto. Last I saw them; they were small white birds flying out of their cages. Now they had morphed into beautiful glowing Venusians. Then as the music grew louder, the fairies began singing. With that, the platform picked up speed and soon the fairies were nothing but a blur whizzing by.

But my brother—where was he? Scanning the sky for Puck and Michael, I couldn't see anything but a clear lilac sky. I thought they were right behind us the whole time. Could they have traveled somewhere else?

"Surprise!" a group of voices shouted as if it were my birthday.

I turned to see Michael, Puck, Celeste and Asea stepping out of the wicker basket attached to the hot air balloon. They must have been hiding from me.

"We beat you," Michael said playfully.

"As usual."

"Thank you so much for freeing my brothers

and sisters. I am forever grateful," Celeste said, her face beaming more than usual. She walked toward me with arms outstretched. "I'll give you anything you want in gratitude."

"I'm afraid you can't give me what I want," I mumbled, glancing at my brother. It had been so long since Michael looked like Michael. Like my big brother. Like the kid who would do anything for me. The ruddy color had returned to his cheeks and the spark of life to his eyes. He stood like a football player, tall with an athletic build, not like a hospital patient wasting away on a rollaway bed. An undeniable joy had taken hold of Michael, something I hadn't witnessed since we were young kids. For the first time I could remember, I wasn't faking happiness for Michael—with envy boiling under the surface of my smile. I was truly happy for him. But I knew we couldn't remain on Venus or at least I couldn't stay. I think that was the hardest part about seeing him so happy. Salty tears stung the corners of my eyes as I thought about the inevitable goodbye. I blinked a few times and looked away before Michael noticed.

I then turned my attention to Puck and Portia. They looked like they had just won the lottery. I think what I noticed first, besides their stunning silver wings, was their perfect posture. No longer did they hunch over like old people pacing the halls in a nursing home. Instead, they stood proud and erect like soldiers. Their silky chocolate manes flowed from their faces, as if they had just been groomed, although they had been flying in the wind. Their reptilian tails, mangy and scaly on Pluto, now shimmered as if made of hundreds of shiny silver dollars. I felt such joy for them, I could barely contain it in my skin, and then I looked at Michael and remembered how temporary my joy was.

"Race you to the Ferris Wheel!" Puck called out.

Together Michael and I ran through the amusement park as if we owned the place. We zipped down the wavy slide, floated on the flume ride, and crashed bumper cars. We rode the carousel horses, piloted planes, and raced run-away trains. Then we did it all over again. When we grew tired of those attractions, Puck and Portia, always a few steps ahead, showed us rides and games we had never heard of. Finally, saving the best for last—we boarded the pyramid roller coaster. I think Michael and I rode the roller coaster thirty-two times before calling it quits. I could not remember a day on earth more fun. But even as I enjoyed myself, I knew it couldn't last. I had to go home and I needed to let Michael know.

After looping around the amusement park several times, I found myself alone with Michael only feet away from the hot air balloon. I could see Celeste laughing with the fairies on the carousel.

"Do you think we're dreaming?" Michael asked, without looking at me.

"How could we both be dreaming the same dream?"

"Could this really be Venus? It's supposed to be cloudy and boiling hot." Michael turned and touched my arm. I couldn't help but face him. He had an otherworldly look—like he was happy and sad at the same time. "Remember when we used to stare through the telescope at night, trying to name the stars? I miss those days," he said.

"Me too."

"You know we could just stay here. We'd never have to worry about school, or money, or getting sick, or—"

"Is that what you want?" I asked, although I didn't want to know the answer.

"I don't know what I want," he replied.

"What about Mom and Dad?" I interrupted. "Don't you want to go home?"

"I have nothing at home. I'm stuck in a bed, where my feet are forever cold and my stomach is forever empty. The only break I get, if you want to call it that, is when I dream. Otherwise, I'm just a shell of a person trapped in a frozen body."

I had wondered for three weeks how Michael felt inside a comatose body and now I knew. But I didn't want to know. Reaching out for his hand, I brushed up against his wrist. His skin felt warm to the touch. "I had no idea, Michael. I'm sorry. I'm so sorry I had to dive into the waves that day. The riptide was bad and I ignored it. If it weren't for me and my selfish decision, my stupidity, you would be okay."

"Don't be sorry. You did nothing wrong. It was my decision to jump in the ocean. I wanted it that way." Michael touched my shoulder and looked directly at me. "I have a secret—a secret place really."

"What place? Where is it?"

"Whenever I'm troubled by something, looking for answers, I visit a secret place in my dreams. At least I think it's a dream."

"Is it the Galactic Library?" I asked.

"Yes! How did you know?"

"I've been there, too. That place scares me."

"I visited it recently. Something happened." Michael looked away. I could hear the tension in his voice. I could almost feel it on my skin.

"What happened?"

"I found myself in a giant rotunda staring up at the ceiling. A young girl greeted me. I realize now she was Celeste. She asked me to transport a crystal back to earth. To bury it."

"That was the crystal Danko had, right?" I interrupted.

"It was. Celeste asked me to view the book of my life in order to determine where to bury the crystal on earth. When I opened the pages of my book, I saw you drowning, but I didn't dive into the ocean. Something stopped me from plunging in to try to save you. You drowned, Jack."

"But you did jump in. You did save me," I insisted.

"Not the first time. The first time was horrific. Mom and Dad moped around the house like zombies. Your funeral, you wouldn't believe it, people came from hundreds of miles away, people we don't even know, to pay their respects. I couldn't take it. The guilt was eating me alive." Michael shuddered. "I slammed the book shut and ran out of the Galactic Library."

"What did Celeste say?"

"I never said goodbye to her or anyone else. I just ran and ran. I had to get home and save you."

"Is that when you dropped half the crystal?" I asked.

"Probably. As I sprinted toward a roller coaster, I held the crystal in my hand. I might have shoved it in my pocket at some point."

"How did you get home?" I asked.

"I don't know. It was a dream. I got on the pyramid roller coaster and woke up in my bed. The crystal—or half of the crystal—was still in my pocket when I got out of bed."

"Was that the day we went down to the shore?"

"No. I had the dream in the beginning of the summer… weeks before my accident. I had forgotten all about it."

"But then you remembered," I added, choking back the tears.

"I couldn't live with myself if anything ever happened to you," Michael said, he was almost whispering. "You didn't do anything wrong."

"I wish you were alive like this on earth, able to speak with me, and play football and laugh. I miss you so much."

"You know I can't board the hot air balloon. I can only return to earth in a dream." Michael stared up at the lilac sky, "I don't know if I can do it."

"What?"

"Go back to a frozen body."

"You don't have to do it for me," I insisted.

"Will you stay here?" Michael begged. "Please."

I knew that question was coming. I had avoided it since we landed on Venus, somehow hoping the amusement park thrills and beautiful scenery would make the question go away. Should I lie, tell him what he wants to hear? I would stay with him. Or tell him the truth? I wanted to go back home to earth with all its imperfections. I desperately wanted him to come home with me, too, but I couldn't make him. Michael had no desire to return to earth and lay motionless in a cold bed. He wanted to run free with horses and swim in crystal clear pools. And I could not stop him. I had no right to guilt him into coming back with me.

We clung to each other for a long time, not saying a word. We didn't have to speak. We both just knew. I think it was at that precise moment I realized it was Michael's decision, not mine. He could return to earth or stay on Venus. I would respect his decision no matter how painful it was for me.

"I'm going back home," I said, figuring there was no point in hiding my true feelings. He could sense them anyway.

"Part of me, most of me, would like to stay here but another part wants to go home, too," Michael admitted.

"You don't have to come back to earth for me." I struggled to swallow over the lump in my throat, muttering, "You can stay on Venus. I'll understand."

"I know." Michael drew his hands to his face and rubbed his eyes with his fingertips. "I haven't made my decision yet. I wish I could go to the Galactic Library and study my book. Maybe I'd get a few answers."

"You can. There's an entrance at the carousel," I told him. "There's a whole world under that carousel. Go see for yourself."

"That's what I'm going to do."

"Have you visited the hologram room?"

"No. What's that?" Michael asked, his forehead wrinkling.

"I think you can project your image out into the universe, but I have no idea how it's done. Ask the librarian. His name is Fagan."

"Can you come with me?" Michael pleaded. "You could show me around."

"I have to go home. I'm afraid I'll never return to earth if I don't board the balloon right now. Besides, I don't want to know anything about the future. I want to live in the present."

Celeste stepped away from the carousel and approached us, her face more radiant than I remembered. Together we walked away from the others in the direction of the hot air balloon and I could feel my heart beating faster. She knew I missed earth, my family, my friends, everything in my little corner of the world.

"I have something for you," she said opening her fist.

"This new twin crystal is for you. I gave Michael the other half," Celeste said, extending her arm out. "You can communicate by thought so long as you each hold your half of the Aphrodite quartz."

"Can I heal him with this crystal?" I begged, my face flushing with heat. "What if I play a recording of the secret music notes?"

"If Michael chooses to return to his three dimensional body, your crystal could activate his

DNA. But there is no guarantee. The future is only a string of possibilities." Celeste smiled at me.

Without saying a word to each other, Michael and I joined our crystals together just as Danko attempted to do in the dungeon before he evaporated. We didn't hesitate. Maybe we should have been frightened but we weren't. As the crystals touched, an electrifying bolt zoomed up my arm assuring me that Michael and I would always be connected. Now I felt better about boarding the hot air balloon.

It was difficult saying farewell to Celeste, Asea and the twins. As we hugged, each of them gave me something to remember them by. In my jean pocket, I had Celeste's Aphrodite quartz, a lucky charm shaped like a horn from Asea, and two silver dollar shells plucked from the twins' tails. The shells sparkled as if soaked in silver glitter glue.

Although it was hard to say goodbye to the Venusians, when you think you're saying farewell to your brother, your best friend, forever and ever, the word goodbye is excruciating. So we didn't say it. We just hugged, neither one of us wanting to be the one to break away first. My heart felt so heavy, I could barely hold it in my chest, but I knew I had to let him go.

CHAPTER 18
Home Again

The hot air balloon, painted in vivid swirls of deep purple, stood proudly before me. This was a far more beautiful balloon than the one I had abandoned on Pluto. As I climbed into the tawny-colored wicker basket, I somehow knew it was my last balloon ride. Hot stinging tears streamed down my cheeks, but I forced a smile.

With one hand stroking the crystal in my pocket, I lifted the other and waved to Michael and the Venusians. They stood crowded around in a circle flapping their wings, waving their arms, and calling out to me. I felt both exhilaration and profound sadness. The doubting words echoing through my head fell silent to the sound of the roaring propane burners. I could jump if I wanted to—I still had time—but I knew I couldn't stay on Venus. Earth was home.

The balloon ascended like a bird taking flight. As the breathtaking view of Venus grew smaller and smaller, the amethyst painted sky muted into a familiar orange-streaked sunset. Now my head and limbs felt heavier, like bags of wet sand, forcing me to sit down in the basket or risk falling. I couldn't hold my drooping body any longer.

Soon the familiar sound of screaming children and blaring carnival music replaced the blast of the

255

propane burners. As the balloon touched ground, shuddering to a halt, a sense of relief passed through me. I struggled to stand up, but my legs went weak like a marionette puppet. Inhaling deeply, I tried once more to get up but slid back down. Clouds floated through my head making it difficult to think clearly. Was I dreaming? No. I couldn't be. I clutched the side of the basket and hoisted my rubbery body into an upright position.

It took a moment for me to realize that I was back on earth. What time was it? The orange and red smudged sky suggested the sun would set in less than an hour, but it seemed days had passed since I last stood in that exact spot. Where was the balloon operator? I recognized the launching field but didn't see the balloon man. Glancing at the balloon, I was startled to see that it appeared exactly the same as when I took off from earth, with glow-in-the-dark stars smattered across the indigo background—as if I had never gone to Venus. All I could figure was that the launching field was some kind of energy vortex. Was I the only person who traveled to Venus on the hot air balloon? Did the balloon man know about my trip? I didn't want to ask him. I'd sneak out of the basket before anyone noticed.

Shaking my legs a few times to circulate the blood, I glanced around to make sure no one was looking at me. Then I hopped out, careful not to disturb the controls. No sooner had I stepped onto the solid earth, when a light hand tapped my right shoulder. I spun around and recognized the balloon man.

"I'm going to test the balloon now. Will I see you in the morning?" he asked.

"No. I've decided not to ride in the balloon tomorrow."

"What?"

"I'm going to pass on the offer, but thank you."

"Why not? You were so excited earlier. Are you nervous about the tear in the balloon envelope? We've fixed it up good. Let me show you," the balloon man babbled, clearly insulted.

"I plan to spend the rest of the weekend with my family. School's starting on Tuesday and it's the last day of summer."

"Maybe next year."

"Maybe," I mumbled.

As I stepped away from the balloon I thought about my brother. I already missed him.

"Hey, Son. How's the goldfish?" a carnival man shouted out at me.

"Goldfish?"

"The fish I gave you."

"Oh. That fish. It died."

"I'll get you another one. A special kind of fish. Wait here." Chuck trotted off and soon returned with a brand new goldfish, but it was blue with an exotic fanned tail. I felt like I had seen it before. Yes, on Pluto. The fish appeared to be a miniature species of the tropical fish swimming in the castle moat.

"What kind of fish is that?" I asked, staring intently at the fish in a clear cream cheese container.

"This is a betta fish. It's quite resilient. It has both gills for getting oxygen from the water and lungs for breathing air. It's the next generation of fish. If the bowl is too dirty, he'll suck in air."

"Sounds perfect for me."

"Send your friends over to my booth, would you?" Chuck asked.

"I will. Thanks."

I walked away steadier on my feet than when I first hopped out of the wicker basket. The groggy feeling clouding my head had nearly vanished, but I still felt like an alien, different from the other kids. Making my way toward the exit, I passed the "Haunted Maze of Madness" only now it was called the "Crystal Labyrinth" in large neon orange letters with a long line of eager kids wrapped around the outside. I watched the kids enjoying the last few breaths of summer. No worries. No homework.

"Jack," a child's voice said from behind me.

I turned around and recognized Bradley. "Did your mom have the baby?" I asked.

"Yeah. It's a girl," he said, with disappointment. "I wish it was a boy."

"I'm sure you'll make a great big brother.

Hey, I got something for you."

I reached into my back pocket and fished out the silver dollar shell Puck had given me. It glistened, not as brightly as on Venus, but it glimmered more than any shell I'd seen on earth. I figured Bradley would like it. "Take this betta fish and the shell and put them in your fish bowl at home," I instructed handing them both to Bradley.

Bradley's eyes widened as he examined the shell closely and then shifted his eyes to the fish. "Will the water change colors when I drop the shell in the bowl?"

"Maybe. You'll have to let me know."

"I won't give the shell or the fish to anyone else," Bradley called out as he scooted off toward his nanny.

I thought about my family. My parents might be worried about me even though I had scribbled a note. Was Michael still in the hospital or back in his room? I'd soon find out.

The walk seemed shorter and the lawns seemed greener. As I approached my house, I observed crowds of people and news cameras on the street. I counted three television news trucks plus two radio station SUV's. I had never witnessed such commotion on my sleepy block. From a distance, it appeared that the people were lined up for something, not single file, more like a mob of people trying to push their way into a free concert. Who were they and what were they doing at my house? My heart sank as I imagined something happening to Michael. Why news cameras? I sprinted toward the mob scene.

"What is this for?" I asked a bald, middle-aged man with dark, old-fashioned glasses.

"There's a crop circle in that cornfield," he said, gesturing toward my backyard. "Where have you been?"

"I was at the carnival today. I didn't hear about it," I answered defensively. "Why is everyone crowding around?"

"People think it's communication from aliens. I think people watch too many movies."

"Why are you here then?" I sassed, embarrassed as soon as I let the words come out.

"I'm just here to make sure I don't miss anything."

I had forgotten all about the crop circle in Mr. Jenkins' yard. Last I heard he wanted to press charges against me for defacing his property. It didn't seem like people were looking for me. Maybe I'd sneak in closer and take a peek.

Somehow I made my way toward the front without angering anyone in line. Mr. Jenkins stood at the top of the line facing me with the biggest grin plastered across his face. He was passing out tickets and collecting money by the fistful.

"Jack! Jack!" he called out, extending his arm toward me.

"What's this, Mr. Jenkins?" I asked.

"Your crop circle is making me rich. Seems the scientific community thinks it might be for real."

"Really? How do they know?"

"The DNA of the ears of corn was altered. They don't think it's a hoax," he said, wiping his sweaty forehead with a twenty dollar bill.

"I told you I didn't do anything wrong."

"Whatever you did, I wish you'd do it again. Can you do it next year, too?"

I just smiled patting my crystal in my pocket. There was no sense in arguing with Mr. Jenkins.

"I'd like to see your crop circle sometime when the crowds die down," I said, turning back toward my house.

"Hopefully, that's not anytime soon," he replied without glancing up.

I walked in the front door of my house. My parents were seated on the sofa. My mother's face looked serene.

"How's Michael?" I asked, holding my breath.

"Much better. Turns out he didn't have pneumonia," my mom said, standing up and walking toward me. "He's upstairs."

"Is he showing any signs of waking up?"

"He wiggled his right toe," my dad responded. "We're hoping that —" he stopped speaking and closed his eyes.

I had to see for myself. I dashed up the steps two at a time and barged into his room. Jamming my fingers in my front pocket, I stroked the crystal. Then, I clasped Michael's right hand in mine, and prayed for some kind of movement.

"Squeeze my hand if you know what I'm saying," I whispered.

At first nothing happened like all the other times I had sprinted into his room only to be disappointed. But something was different this time. Maybe I was different. A shock, a wave of energy, sparked between us as if I walked across carpet and touched metal. I pinched my eyes shut, painted a vivid image of Venus in my mind, and slowly inhaled. I could feel a slight squeeze against the palm of my hand.

"Michael? Is that you?"

Again, the distinct pressure of his fingers pressing against my palm startled me. I wasn't imagining things. I definitely wasn't dreaming. He did respond to my squeeze. I grabbed his other hand and repeated the request. The squeeze back was even stronger this time.

I opened my eyes and glared out the window at the sky. The sun was setting over the cornfields. Soon rays of moonlight would stream in Michael's window. Buckets of tears clogged up for weeks began gushing down my face. I sobbed and sobbed, and when I couldn't cry anymore I pulled the twin crystal out of my pocket and held it up to the window watching patterns of light dance across my sweaty palm. In the kitchen, I could hear my mom calling me down for dinner.

Michael was coming home.

Ann Tufariello lives in Chatham, New Jersey with her husband and three children. If you would like the author to visit your school in person or online, please visit her website at www.anntufariello.com. Ann loves meeting teachers and students and talking about the writing process.